Maigret and
the Burglar's Wife

GEORGES SIMENON

Maigret and the Burglar's Wife

Translated by J. Maclaren-Ross

A Harvest/HBJ Book
A Helen and Kurt Wolff Book
Harcourt Brace Jovanovich, Publishers
San Diego   New York   London

HBJ

Copyright © 1956, 1955 by Georges Simenon
Copyright renewed 1984, 1983 by Georges Simenon

Originally published as
Maigret et la grande perche in France, 1951.

Library of Congress Cataloging-in-Publication Data
Simenon, Georges, 1903–1989.
[Maigret et la grande perche. English]
Maigret and the burglar's wife / Georges Simenon ;
translated by J. Maclaren-Ross. — 1st ed.
p.   cm.
Translation of: Maigret et la grande perche.
"A Helen and Kurt Wolff book."
ISBN 0-15-155572-9
ISBN 0-15-655167-5 (pbk.)
I. Title.
PQ2637.I53M25713   1990
843'.912—dc20   89-15625

Designed by Kaelin Chappell
Printed in the United States of America
First Harvest/HBJ edition 1991

A B C D E

Maigret and
the Burglar's Wife

1

The official slip of paper, duly filled in and handed to Maigret by the office boy, read:

Ernestine Micou, alias Lofty (now Jussiaume), who, when you arrested her seventeen years ago on rue de la Lune, stripped herself naked to taunt you, requests the favor of an interview on a matter of most urgent and important business.

Maigret glanced quickly out of the corner of his eye at old Joseph, to see whether he'd read the message, but the white-haired "office boy" didn't move a muscle. He was probably the only one in the whole of the Police Judiciaire that morning who wasn't in shirtsleeves, and for the first time in many years the Chief Inspector wondered by what official vagary this almost venerable man was compelled to wear around his neck a heavy chain with a huge seal.

It was the sort of day when one is apt to indulge in pointless speculation. The heat wave may have been to blame. Perhaps the vacation spirit also prevented one from taking things very seriously. The windows were wide open, and the muted roar of Paris throbbed in the room, where, before Joseph came in, Maigret had been engaged in following the flight of a wasp, which was going around in circles and bumping against the ceiling invariably at the same spot. At least half of the inspectors were either at the seaside or in the country. Lucas went wearing a straw hat, which, on him, looked like a native grass hat or a lampshade. The Big Chief had left the day before for the Pyrenees, where he went year after year.

"Drunk?" Maigret asked Joseph.

"Don't think so, sir."

A certain type of woman, having taken a drop too much, often feels impelled to make disclosures to the police.

"Nervous?"

"She asked me if it would be long, and I said I didn't even know if you'd see her. She sat herself down in a corner of the waiting room and started to read the paper."

Maigret couldn't recall the names Micou or Jussiaume, or the nickname Lofty, but he retained a vivid memory of rue de la Lune, on a day as hot as this, when the asphalt feels elastic underfoot and fills Paris with the smell of tar.

It was near Porte St.-Denis, a little street of dubious hotels and small pastry shops. He wasn't a chief inspector in those days. The women wore low-cut dresses and had bobbed hair. To find out about this girl, he'd had to go into two or three neighborhood bistros, and he'd been drinking Pernod. He could almost conjure up the smell of it, just as he could conjure up the smell of armpits and feet pervading the small hotel. The room was on the fourth or fifth floor. Choosing the wrong door, he'd found himself face to face with a black man sitting on the bed and playing the accordion: a member of the band in a *bal musette*, probably. Quite unperturbed, the man had indicated the room next door with a jerk of his chin.

"Come in!"

A husky voice, the voice of one who drank or smoked too much. Standing by a window that opened on the court-yard was a girl in a sky-blue dressing gown, cooking a chop on an alcohol stove.

She was taller than Maigret. She'd looked him up and down with no expression and said: "You're a cop?"

He'd found the wallet and the money on top of the wardrobe; she hadn't batted an eyelid.

"It was my girlfriend who did it."

"What girlfriend?"

"Don't know her name. . . . Lulu, they call her."

"Where is she?"

"Find out. That's your business."

"Get dressed and come with me."

It was only a case of petty theft, but the Police Judiciaire took a serious view of it—not so much because of the sum involved, though it was pretty large, but because it was taken from a big cattle dealer from the Charente, who had already stirred up his local deputy.

3

"It'll take more than you to keep me from eating my chop!"

The tiny room contained only one chair, so he'd remained standing while the girl ate, taking her time. He might not have been there, for all the attention she paid him.

She must have been about twenty at the time. She was pale, with colorless eyes and a long bony face. He could see her now, picking her teeth with a matchstick and pouring boiling water into the coffeepot.

"I asked you to get dressed."

He was hot. The smell of the hotel turned his stomach. Had she sensed that he was ill at ease?

Calmly, she'd taken off her dressing gown, her slip and panties. Stark naked, she'd lain down on the unmade bed and lit a cigarette.

"I'm waiting!" he'd told her impatiently, looking away with an effort.

"So am I."

"I have a warrant for your arrest."

"Well, arrest me, then!"

"Get dressed and come along."

"I'm all right like this."

The whole thing was ludicrous. She was cool, quite passive, only a little glint of irony showing in her colorless eyes.

"You say I'm under arrest. *I* don't mind. But you needn't ask me to give you a hand. I'm in my own place. It's hot, and I have a right to take my clothes off. If you insist that I go with you, just as I am, I won't complain."

4

At least a dozen times he'd told her: "Get your things on!"

And, perhaps because of her pale flesh, perhaps because of the surrounding squalor, it seemed to him that he'd never seen a woman so naked. He'd thrown her clothes on the bed, threatened her, tried persuasion, to no avail.

Finally, he'd gone down and called two policemen, and the scene became absurd. They'd had to wrap the girl forcibly in a blanket and carry her, like a package, down the narrow staircase, and all the doors opened as they went by.

He'd never seen her since. He'd never heard her mentioned.

"Send her in!" He sighed.

He knew her at once. She didn't seem to have changed. He recognized her long pale face, the washed-out eyes, the big lipsticked mouth, which looked like a raw wound. He recognized also, in her glance, the quiet irony of those who have seen so much that nothing's any longer important in their eyes.

She was simply dressed, wore a light-green straw hat, and had put on gloves.

"Still got it in for me?"

He drew on his pipe without answering.

"Can I sit down? I heard you'd been promoted, and that's why I never ran into you again. Is it all right if I smoke?"

She took a cigarette from her bag and lit it.

"I want to tell you right away, with no hard feelings, that I was telling the truth that time. I got a year I didn't deserve. There was a girl called Lulu, all right, but you

5

didn't take the trouble to find her. . . . The two of us were together when we ran across that fat slob. He picked us both up, but when he took a good look at me, he told me to get going, because he couldn't stand 'em skinny. I was outside in the hall when Lulu slipped me the wallet an hour after, so I could ditch it."

"What became of her?"

"Five years ago she had a little restaurant down south. . . . I just wanted to show you everyone sometimes makes mistakes."

"Is that why you came?"

"No. I wanted to talk to you about Alfred. If he knew I was here, he'd think I was crazy. I could've gone to Inspector Boissier; the inspector knows all about him."

"Who's Alfred?"

"My husband. Lawfully wedded, too, before the mayor *and* the vicar, because he still goes to church. Boissier's picked him up two or three times. And one of those times he got Alfred five years in Fresnes."

Her voice was almost harsh.

"The name Jussiaume doesn't mean much to you, maybe, but when I tell you what they call him, you'll know who he is right away. There's been a lot about him in the papers. . . . He's Sad Freddie."

"Safecracker?"

"Yes."

"You've had a fight?"

"No. It's not what you think I've come for. I'm not that sort. . . . So you know who Fred is now?"

Maigret had never met him, but had seen him in the corridors of the PJ when the safecracker was waiting to be

6

interrogated by Boissier. He vaguely recalled a puny little man with anxious eyes, whose clothes seemed too big for his scrawny body.

"Of course, we don't look at him the same way," she said. "Poor dope. There's more to him than you think. I've lived with him nearly twelve years, and I'm only starting to get to know him."

"Where is he?"

"I'm coming to that, don't worry. . . . I don't know where he is, but he's in a jam, and it's not his fault. That's why I'm here. But you've got to trust me, and I know that's asking a lot."

He was watching her with interest, because she spoke with appealing simplicity. She wasn't putting on airs, wasn't trying to impress him. If she took some time in coming to the point, it was because what she had to tell was genuinely complicated.

There was still a barrier between them, nevertheless, and it was this barrier she was trying hard to break down, so he wouldn't get the wrong idea of things.

About Sad Freddie, with whom he'd never had any personal dealings, Maigret knew little more than what he'd heard around the PJ. The man was somewhat of a celebrity, and the newspapers had tried their best to turn him into a romantic figure.

He had been employed for years by Planchart, the big safe-making firm, and had become one of their most skilled workers. He was, even at that time, a sad, retiring youth, in poor health and subject to epileptic fits.

Boissier would probably be able to tell Maigret how he had come to give up his job at Planchart.

Whatever the cause, Sad Freddie had turned from installing safes to cracking them.

"When you first met him, did he still have a steady job?"

"No . . . It wasn't me that sent him off the straight and narrow, in case that's what you're thinking. He was doing odd jobs. Sometimes he'd work for a locksmith. . . . But it wasn't long before I saw what he was really up to."

"You don't think you'd do better to see Boissier?"

"Housebreaking's his line, isn't it? You're the one who deals with murder."

"Has Alfred killed somebody?"

"Look, Chief Inspector, I think we'll get along faster if you just let me talk. . . . Alfred may be anything you want to call him, but he wouldn't murder for all the money in the world. It may seem soppy to say this about a fellow like him, but he's sensitive. . . . I ought to know. Anyone else would say he was soft. But that was the reason I fell in love with him."

She looked at him quietly. She'd uttered the word "love" without particular emphasis, yet with a sort of pride.

"If you knew what was going on in his head, you wouldn't be surprised. . . . Not that it matters. Far as you're concerned, he's just a thief who got himself picked up once and did five years. . . .

"I never missed a single visiting day, and all that time I had to go back to my old beat, at the risk of getting in trouble . . . not having a card, and that was when you still had to have one. . . .

"He always hopes he'll pull off a big job, and then we can go live in the country. He's always dreamed of it, ever since he was little."

"Where do you live?"

"On Quai de Jemmapes, opposite the St. Martin lock. Know where I mean? . . . We've got two rooms over a café, painted green, and it's very handy because of the phone."

"Is Alfred there now?"

"No. I already told you I don't know where he is, and, believe me, I don't. He did a job—not last night, but the night before."

"And he's disappeared?"

"Hang on, will you, Chief Inspector! You'll see later on that everything I'm telling you has a point.

"You know people who buy national lottery tickets for every draw, don't you? Some of them go without eating to buy them, because they figure that in a day or two they'll be in the money at last. Well, that's the way it is with Alfred. There are dozens of safes in Paris that he installed himself, safes he knows like the back of his hand. Usually when you buy a safe, it's to put money or jewels away in."

"He hopes to strike it lucky someday?"

"That's it." She shrugged, as though speaking of a child's harmless enthusiasm.

Then she added: "He's just unlucky. Most times all he gets are title deeds you can't sell, or business contracts. Only once was there big money, money he could have lived on quietly for the rest of his days. And that was the time Boissier caught him."

"Were you with him? Are you the lookout?"

"No. He never liked me to . . . In the beginning, he used to tell me where he was going, and I'd fix it so I was nearby. When he spotted that, he stopped telling me anything."

9

"Afraid you'd get caught?"

"Maybe. Or maybe because he's superstitious . . . See, even when we're together, he's all alone really. Sometimes he doesn't say a word for two whole days. . . . When I see him go out at night on his bicycle, I know what's up."

Maigret remembered that some of the newspapers had dubbed Alfred Jussiaume "the burglar-on-a-bike."

"That's another of his notions. He thinks that nobody, at night, is going to notice a man on a bicycle, especially if he's got a bag of tools over his shoulder. That they'll think he's on his way to work. . . . I'm talking to you like I would to a friend, see?"

Maigret wondered again why she had come. When she took out another cigarette, he held a lighted match for her.

"Today's Thursday. On Tuesday night, Alfred went out on a job."

"Did he tell you so?"

"Well, he'd been going out for several nights just before, and that's always a sign. Before he breaks into a house or an office, he sometimes spends a week watching, to get to know the people's habits."

"And to make sure there'll be no one around?"

"No. That doesn't matter to him. I think he'd rather work where there *was* somebody, instead of in an empty house. He can move around without making a sound. Why, hundreds of times he's slipped into bed beside me at night and I never so much as knew he'd come home."

"Do you know where he worked night before last?"

"All I know is it was in Neuilly. And I only found that out by chance. . . . The day before, when I came in, he told me the police had asked to see his papers, and he

10

thought they must've taken him for a dirty old man, because they stopped him in the Bois de Boulogne, right by the place where women go and clean up.

" 'Where was it?' I asked him.

" 'Behind the zoo. I was coming back from Neuilly.'

"Then, night before last, he took his bag of tools, and I knew he'd gone to work."

"He hadn't been drinking?"

"Never touches a drop. Doesn't smoke. He's never been able to. He's afraid of his fits, and he's ashamed when one happens in the middle of the street, where people crowd around and feel sorry for him. . . .

"Before he left, he said: 'I think this time we're really going to live in the country.' "

Maigret had begun to take notes, which he was surrounding idly with arabesques.

"What time did he leave Quai de Jemmapes?"

"About eleven, like he did on the other nights."

"Then he must have got to Neuilly around midnight."

"Maybe. He never rode fast. But at that time, there'd be no traffic."

"When did you see him again?"

"I haven't seen him again."

"So you think something may have happened to him?"

"He telephoned me."

"When?"

"Five in the morning . . . I wasn't asleep. I was worried. If he's always afraid he'll have a fit in the street, I'm always afraid it might happen while he's working. Anyway, I heard the phone ringing downstairs in the café. Our room's right above. The owners didn't get up, so I guessed it might be

11

for me, and I went down. I knew right away from his voice there'd been a hitch. He talked very low.

" 'That you?'

" 'Yes!'

" 'Are you alone?'

" 'Yes. Where are you?'

" 'In a little bistro by Gare du Nord. . . . Look, Tine'— he always calls me Tine—'I've got to go away for a while.'

" 'Somebody see you?'

" 'It's not that. . . . I don't know. . . . A man saw me, yes. But I don't think it was a policeman.'

" 'Get any money?'

" 'No. It happened before I'd finished.'

" '*What* happened?'

" 'I was busy on the lock when my flashlight fell on a face in a corner. . . . I thought somebody had come in and was watching me. Then I saw the eyes were dead.' "

She watched Maigret.

"I'm sure he wasn't lying. If he'd killed someone, he'd have told me. . . . And I'm not making stories up for you. I could tell he was almost passing out. He's so scared of corpses. . . ."

"What sort of person was it?"

"I don't know. He didn't make it very clear. He kept wanting to hang up, because he was afraid somebody'd hear him. He told me he was taking a train in a quarter of an hour—"

"To Belgium?"

"Probably, since he was near Gare du Nord. . . . I looked at a timetable. There's a train at five-forty-five."

"Do you have any idea what bistro he was calling from?"

12

"I scouted around the district yesterday and asked some questions. But no good. They must've taken me for a jealous wife; they weren't going to give anything away."

"So all he really told you was that there was a dead body in the room where he was working?"

"I got him to tell me a little more. He said it was a woman, that her chest was covered with blood, and that she was holding a telephone in her hand."

"Is that all?"

"No. Just as he was about to run—and I can imagine the state he was in!—a car drove up in front of the gate."

"You're sure he said the gate?"

"Yes. A wrought-iron gate. I remember it struck me particularly. A man got out and came toward the door. When he entered the hallway, Alfred went out through the window."

"His tools?"

"He left them behind. . . . He'd cut out a windowpane to get in. That I'm sure of, because he always does. He'd probably do it even if the door was open; he's sort of a stickler, or maybe superstitious."

"The man saw him?"

"Bad luck. As he was going through the garden—"

"He mentioned a garden?"

"I didn't make it up! Just as he was going through the garden, someone looked out the window and turned a flashlight on him. Maybe Alfred's, since he'd left his behind. He jumped on his bicycle and, without looking around, rode down as far as the Seine—I don't know exactly where. He threw the bike in, in case he could be recognized by it. . . . He didn't dare come back home, so he walked to

13

Gare du Nord and called me, telling me not to say a word.

"I begged him not to run away. I tried to reason with him. He did promise to write me, poste restante, saying where he'd be, so I could join him."

"He hasn't written yet?"

"There hasn't been time for a letter to get here, though I did go to the post office this morning. . . . I've had twenty-four hours to think things over. I bought all the papers, thinking there'd surely be something about a murdered woman."

Maigret picked up the telephone and called the Neuilly police.

"Hello! This is the PJ. . . . Any murder during the last twenty-four hours?"

"One moment, sir. I'll get you the desk."

Maigret spent some time asking questions.

"No corpse found on the street? . . . No night calls? No bodies fished out of the Seine?"

"Absolutely nothing, Chief."

"Nobody reported a shot?"

"No."

Lofty waited patiently, like someone making a social call, both hands clasped on her bag.

"You realize why I came to *you*?"

"I think so."

"First, I thought the police had maybe seen Alfred, and in that case his bicycle would have given him away. Then there were the tools he left behind. Now that he's bolted over the border, no one'll ever believe his story. . . . And he's no safer in Belgium or Holland than in Paris. I'd sooner see him in jail for attempted burglary, even if it meant five years all over again, than see him up for murder."

"The trouble is, there's no body," Maigret said.

"You think he made it up? Or I'm making it up?"

He didn't answer.

"It'll be easy for you to find the house he was working in. Maybe I shouldn't tell you this—I'm sure you'll think of it yourself—but the safe's bound to be one of those he put in. Planchart must keep a list of customers, and there can't be that many in Neuilly who bought a safe at least seventeen years ago."

"Besides you, did Alfred have any girlfriends?"

"Ah! I guessed that was coming. . . . I'm not jealous. And even if I was, I wouldn't come to you with a pack of lies to get him back, if that's what you have in mind. He doesn't have a girlfriend because he doesn't want one, the poor dope. If he wanted one, I'd fix him up, with as many as he liked."

"Why?"

"Because life's not much fun for him, as it is."

"Have you any money?"

"No."

"What are you going to do?"

"I'll get by, as you well know. I came here only because I want you to prove that Freddie didn't kill anyone."

"If he wrote to you, would you show me his letter?"

"You'll read it before I do. Now that you know he's going to write me poste restante, you'll have every post office in Paris watched. You forget that I know your tricks."

She had risen to her feet; very tall, she looked him over as he sat at his desk.

"If all the stories they tell about you are true, there's an even chance you'll believe me."

"Why?"

"Because otherwise you'd be a fool. And you're not one. Are you going to call Planchart?"

"Yes."

"You'll let me know?"

He looked at her without replying, but couldn't stop himself from giving her a good-humored smile.

"Please yourself, then." She sighed. "I could help you. You may know an awful lot, but there're things people like us understand better than you do."

Her "us" obviously stood for a whole world, the one that Lofty lived in, a world on the other side of a barrier.

"If Inspector Boissier's not on vacation, I'm sure he'll back up what I told you about Alfred."

"He's not going until tomorrow."

She opened her bag and took out a piece of paper.

"I'll leave you the phone number of the café under where we live. If, by some chance, you need to come see me, don't be afraid I'll start undressing. Nowadays, if it's left to me, I keep my clothes on!"

There was a touch of bitterness in her tone, but not much. A second later she was poking fun at herself: "Much better for all concerned!"

It wasn't until he closed the door behind her that Maigret realized he had, quite as a matter of course, shaken the hand she'd held out to him. The wasp was still buzzing in circles near the ceiling, as though looking for a way out, never thinking of the wide-open windows. Madame Maigret had announced that morning that she'd be coming to the flower market and had asked him, if he was free about noon, to meet her there. It was noon now. He paused, uncertain, then leaned out the window, from which he could see splashes of vivid color.

He picked up the telephone with a sigh.

"Ask Boissier to come see me."

Seventeen years had slipped by since the absurd incident on rue de la Lune, and Maigret was now an important official, in charge of Criminal Investigation. A funny notion came into his head, an almost childish craving. He picked up the telephone once more.

"Brasserie Dauphine, please."

As the door opened to admit Boissier, he was saying: "Send up a Pernod, will you?"

Looking at the Inspector, who had large half-moons of sweat on his shirt underneath his arms, he changed it to: "Make it two! Two Pernods. Thank you."

Boissier's blue-black mustache twitched with pleasure as he went over to sit on the windowsill, mopping his forehead.

2

After swallowing a mouthful of Pernod, Maigret came to the point.

"Tell me, Boissier, what you know about Alfred Jussiaume."

"Sad Freddie?"

"Yes."

Immediately the Inspector's brow darkened. He shot Maigret a worried glance and asked, in a voice no longer the same, and forgetting to take a sip of his favorite drink: "Has he pulled off a job?"

It was always like this with him, Maigret knew. He also knew why, and, by using the utmost tact, had become the only chief inspector to find favor in Boissier's eyes.

18

The latter, by rights, ought to have been one himself, and would have been a long time ago, except for an absolute inability to spell and the handwriting of a schoolboy, which prevented him from passing the simplest examinations.

For once, however, the administrative staff had not made a mistake. They had appointed Chief Inspector Peuchet, an old has-been, always half asleep, as head of Boissier's division, knowing that, except for writing reports, it would be Boissier who got through all the work and supervised his colleagues.

That division wasn't concerned with homicide, as Maigret's was. It wasn't concerned with amateurs either—like sales clerks who ran off one fine day with the money in the till, or anything of that sort.

The customers Boissier and his men dealt with were professional thieves of every kind, from jewel robbers who stayed at the big hotels on the Champs Elysées to bank robbers and con men who hid out mostly, like Jussiaume, in seedy neighborhoods.

Because of this, they had an outlook quite different from that of the Crime Squad. In Boissier's line, they were all professionals on both sides. The battle was a battle between experts. It wasn't so much a question of psychology, as of knowing, from A to Z, the little quirks and eccentricities of everyone.

It was not unusual to see the Inspector sitting quietly outside a café with a cat burglar, and Maigret, for one, would have found it hard to hold a conversation such as they were having, with a murderer:

"Julot, it's a long time since you did a job."

"That's right, Inspector."

19

"When was the last time I pulled you in?"

"Must be going on six months, now."

"Funds getting low, eh? I'll bet you're cooking something up."

The idea that Sad Freddie might have planned something or done something without his knowledge upset Boissier.

"I don't know if he's really been on the job lately, but Lofty has just left my office."

That was enough to reassure Boissier.

"She doesn't know a thing," he stated. "Alfred's not the type to go blabbing his business to a woman, not even his own wife."

The picture of Jussiaume that Boissier proceeded to draw was not really different from the one outlined by Ernestine, even though he tended to emphasize the professional angle.

"I get fed up with arresting a fellow like that and sending him to prison. Last time, when they dished out five years to him, I damn near gave his lawyer a piece of my mind for not knowing how to do his job. He's lacking, that lawyer is!"

It was hard to define precisely what Boissier meant by "lacking," but the point was plain enough.

"There's not another man in Paris like Alfred for breaking into a house full of people without a sound and going to work without even waking the cat. Technically, he's an artist. What's more, he doesn't need anyone to tip him off, keep a lookout, and all that. He works on his own, without ever getting jumpy. He doesn't drink, doesn't talk, doesn't act tough around people. With his talents, he ought to have enough money to choke himself with. He knows just where to find hundreds of safes that he put in himself, and

20

exactly how they work, and you'd think he'd only have to go and help himself. Instead, every time he tries, he messes up, or else gets peanuts."

Perhaps Boissier spoke this way only because he saw a parallel between Sad Freddie's career and his own, except that he enjoyed a constitution that could withstand any number of drinks on café terraces and nights spent on watch in all kinds of weather.

"The joke is that, even if they put him away for ten years or twenty years, he'd start all over again as soon as he got out. He'd do it even if he was seventy and on crutches. He's got it into his head that he needs only one lucky break, just one, and that he's earned it by this time."

"He's had a nasty knock," Maigret explained. "It seems that he was just getting a safe open, somewhere in Neuilly, when he spotted a dead body in the room."

"What'd I tell you? That could happen only to him. Then he ran off? What'd he do with the bike?"

"In the Seine."

"He's in Belgium?"

"Probably."

"I'll call Brussels, unless you don't want him picked up."

"I want him picked up most decidedly."

"Do you know where it happened?"

"I know that it was in Neuilly, and that the house has a garden with a wrought-iron gate in front."

"That'll be easy. . . . Be back right away."

Maigret had the grace to order, in his absence, two more Pernods from the Brasserie Dauphine. It brought back to him not only a whiff of the rue de la Lune period, but also a whiff of the South of France, particularly of a little dive

21

in Cannes, where he'd once been on a case and, all of a sudden, the whole affair was lifted out of the general rut and took on a holiday aspect.

He hadn't definitely promised Madame Maigret to meet her in the flower market, and she knew that she must never wait for him.

Boissier returned with a file, from which he produced, first of all, the official photographs of Alfred Jussiaume.

"That's what he looks like!"

An ascetic face, really, rather than that of a street boy. The skin was stretched tight across the bones, the nostrils were long and pinched, and the stare had an almost mystical intensity. Even in these harshly lit photographs, full face and side view, collarless, showing a prominent Adam's apple, the man's immense loneliness could be felt, and a sadness that was in no way aggressive.

It had been natural for Jussiaume, a born victim, to be hunted.

"Would you like me to read you his record?"

"It's not necessary. I'd rather go over the file with an open mind. What I'd like to have is the list of safes."

Boissier was pleased by this. Maigret knew that he would be, as he said it; he'd intended it as a tribute to the Inspector.

"You knew I'd have it?"

"I was sure you would."

Because Boissier really did know his job. The list in question was that, drawn from Planchart's books, of the safes installed in Alfred Jussiaume's time.

"Wait till I look up Neuilly. You're sure it's Neuilly?"

"I have Ernestine's word for it."

22

"You know, she wasn't really so dumb to come and look you up. But why you?"

"Because I arrested her sixteen or seventeen years ago, and she made a fool of me."

This didn't surprise Boissier; it was all part of the game. They both knew where they stood. The pale-colored Pernod could be smelled throughout the office, inciting the wasp to a kind of frenzy.

"A bank . . . It's certainly not that. Freddie never took to banks; he's leery of the burglar alarms. . . . An oil company, but that's been out of business for ten years . . . A perfume manufacturer . . . he went bankrupt a year ago."

Boissier's finger came to a stop finally on a name, on an address.

"Guillaume Serre, dentist, 43b, rue de la Ferme, Neuilly. You know it? It's just past the zoo, a street parallel to Boulevard Richard-Wallace."

"I know it."

They looked at each other.

"Busy?" asked Maigret.

He was again deliberately feeding Boissier's self-esteem.

"I was just classifying some files. I'm off to Brittany tomorrow."

"Shall we go?"

"I'll get my jacket. Shall I call Brussels first?"

"Yes. And Amsterdam."

"All right."

They went by bus, standing on the open rear platform. On rue de la Ferme, which seemed quiet and countrified, they found a little bistro with four tables on the terrace, between potted green plants, and sat down for lunch.

23

Inside were three bricklayers in white smocks, drinking red wine with their meal. Flies circled around Maigret and Boissier. Farther along, on the other side of the street, they could see a black wrought-iron gate, which should correspond with 43b.

They weren't in any hurry. If there had really been a body in the house, the murderer had had more than twenty-four hours in which to get rid of it.

A waitress in a black dress and a white apron looked after them, but the proprietor came out to greet them, too.

"Nice weather, gentlemen."

"Yes, indeed . . . Would you, by any chance, know of a dentist anywhere around here?"

A sideward nod.

"There's one opposite, over there, but I don't know what he's like. My wife prefers to go to one on Boulevard Sébastopol. This one would be expensive, I'd say. He doesn't have all that many patients."

"Do you know him?"

"A little."

The proprietor paused, looking them over, particularly Boissier.

"You're police, eh?"

Maigret thought it better to say yes.

"Has he done something?"

"We're just making a few inquiries. . . . What does he look like?"

"Taller and bigger than I am, or you," he said, looking this time at the Chief Inspector. "He must be all of two hundred and thirty pounds."

"How old?"

24

"Fifty? Around that anyway. Not too well turned out—which is odd, him being a dentist. Shabby, like old bachelors get."

"He isn't married?"

"Wait a minute. . . . Matter of fact, if I remember rightly, he did get married, about two years ago. . . . There's an old woman living in the house, too—his mother, I suppose—who does the shopping every morning. . . ."

"No maid?"

"Only a daily woman. Mind you, I'm not sure. I only know him because he comes in here now and then for a drink on the sly."

"On the sly?"

"People like him don't come to places like this as a rule. When he does, he always takes a quick look at his house, as if to make sure he can't be seen. And he looks sheepish when he comes up to the counter.

" 'Glass of red wine!' he'll say.

"Never takes anything else. I know by now not to put the bottle back on the shelf, because he's bound to have another. He gulps it, wipes his mouth, and has the change all ready in his hand."

"Does he ever get drunk?"

"Never. Just the two glasses. As he goes out, I see him slip a cachou or a clove into his mouth. So his breath won't smell of wine, of course."

"What's his mother like?"

"A little old woman, very dried up, dressed in black. She never passes the time of day with anybody. And she doesn't look easy to get on with."

"His wife?"

25

"I've hardly seen her except when they go by in the car. But I've heard she's a foreigner. She's tall and stout like him, with a ruddy face."

"Do you think they're away on vacation?"

"Let's see . . . I believe I served him his two glasses of red two or three days ago."

"Two or three?"

"Wait a minute. It was the night the plumber came to mend the beer pump. I'll go ask my wife—to make sure I'm not talking through my hat."

It was two days before—in other words, Tuesday—several hours before Alfred Jussiaume discovered a dead woman's body in the house.

"Can you remember the time?"

"He comes, usually, about half past six."

"On foot?"

"Yes. They've got an old car, but that's the time of day he takes his constitutional. . . . You can't tell me what this is all about?"

"It's not about anything at all. Just checking."

The man didn't believe them; you could see it plainly in his eyes.

"You'll be back?"

Then he turned to the Chief Inspector. "You're not Monsieur Maigret, by any chance, are you?"

"Did someone say so?"

"One of the bricklayers thought he recognized you. If you are, my wife would be very happy to meet you in the flesh."

"We'll be back," he promised.

They'd had a good meal, and they'd drunk the calvados

26

the proprietor, who came from Falaise, had offered them. Now they were walking down the sidewalk on the shady side of the street. Maigret was taking little puffs at his pipe. Boissier had lit a cigarette; two fingers of his right hand were stained as brown as a meerschaum pipe.

They could have been fifty miles outside Paris, in almost any small town. There were more private houses than apartment buildings; some were big middle-class family mansions, a century or more old.

There was only one gate along the street, a black wrought-iron one, beyond which a lawn spread like a green carpet in the sunshine. The brass plate read:

GUILLAUME SERRE
Dental Surgeon

And, in smaller letters:

From 2 to 5 p.m.
By appointment only

The sun struck full on the façade of the house, warming its yellowish stone. Except for two of the windows, the shutters were closed. Boissier could sense that Maigret was undecided.

"Are we going in?"

"What have we got to lose?"

Before crossing the street, he cast a quick glance up and down, and suddenly frowned. Boissier looked toward where Maigret was staring.

"Lofty!" he exclaimed.

She'd just come from Boulevard Richard-Wallace, wearing the same green hat she'd had on that morning. Catching

27

sight of Maigret and Boissier, she paused for a moment, then made straight for them.

"Surprised to see me?"

"How'd you get hold of the address?"

"I called your office about half an hour ago. I wanted to tell you that I found the list. . . . I knew it must be somewhere around. I've seen Alfred looking at it, and putting in crosses here and there. When I left your office this morning, I thought of a place where he might have hidden it."

"Where?"

"Do I have to tell you?"

"It might be better."

"I'd rather not. Not right away."

"What else did you find?"

"How do you know I found anything else?"

"You had no money this morning, and you came here by taxi."

"You're right. There was some money."

"A lot?"

"More than I expected."

"Where's the list?"

"I burned it."

"Why?"

"Because of the crosses. They might have marked places where Alfred worked. And, no matter what, I'm not going to give you evidence against him."

She glanced at the house.

"You going in?"

Maigret nodded.

"Do you mind if I wait for you at that bistro?"

28

She hadn't said a word to Boissier, who was staring at her rather sternly.

"Please yourself," Maigret told her.

Followed by the Inspector, he crossed from the shade into the sunlight, while the tall figure of Ernestine moved off toward the terrace.

It was ten minutes after two. Unless the dentist had gone on vacation, he ought to be, according to the brass plate, waiting for patients in his office. There was an electric bell push on the right of the gateway. Maigret pressed it, and the gate swung open automatically. They crossed the small garden and found another bell push by the front door, which was not mechanically operated. After the peal of the bell inside, there was a long silence. The two men listened, both of them aware that someone was lurking on the other side of the panel; they looked at each other. At last a chain was unhooked, the bolt withdrawn, and a thin crack showed around the door.

"Have you an appointment?"

"We'd like to speak to Monsieur Serre."

"He sees people only by appointment."

The crack did not widen. They could dimly make out a silhouette and the thin face of an old woman.

"According to the brass plate—"

"The plate is twenty-five years old."

"Would you tell your son that Chief Inspector Maigret wishes to see him?"

It was a moment or two before the door opened, revealing a wide hallway with a black-and-white tessellated floor, which resembled that of a convent. The old lady who stood back to let them enter would not have looked out of place in a nun's garb.

"You must excuse me, Chief Inspector, but my son doesn't really care to receive patients off the street."

The woman was far from unpresentable. With a remarkable innate elegance and dignity, she was attempting to efface by her smile any bad impression she might have created.

"Do please come in. . . . I'm afraid I'll have to ask you to wait a bit. For some years my son has been accustomed, especially in summer, to take a siesta, and he's still lying down. If you'd come this way . . ."

She opened a pair of polished oak doors to the left, and Maigret was reminded more than ever of a convent, or a rich parsonage. The faint but insidious smell reminded him of something else; he didn't know what. The drawing room she showed them into was lit only by daylight seeping through the shutters; to enter it from outside was like stepping into a cool bath. And surely the noises of the city could never penetrate this far.

It was as if the house and everything in it had remained unchanged for more than a century, as if the tapestry-covered chairs, the occasional tables, the piano, and the ornaments had always stood in the same places. Even the large photographs on the walls, in black wooden frames, looked like pictures from the time of Nadar. Above the mantelpiece was a man bound by a collar of the last century and wearing bushy side whiskers; on the opposite wall, a woman, about forty, her hair parted in the middle, looked like the Empress Eugénie.

The old lady, who might almost have stepped out of one

of those frames, hovered by them, motioned to chairs, and folded her hands like a Sister of Mercy.

"I don't wish to seem inquisitive, Chief Inspector. My son has no secrets from me. We've never lived apart, although he's now past fifty. I haven't the slightest idea of what brings you here. Before going to disturb him, I would like to know . . ."

She left the sentence unfinished, glancing from one to the other with a gracious smile.

"Your son is married, I believe?"

"He's been married twice."

"Is his second wife at home?"

A shade of melancholy clouded her eyes. Boissier began to cross and uncross his legs; this was not the sort of place he felt at home in.

"She's no longer with us, Chief Inspector."

She moved softly over to close the door. Returning, she sat down in the corner of a sofa, keeping her back very straight, as young girls are taught to do in convent schools.

"I hope she hasn't done anything silly," she said in a low voice.

When Maigret remained silent, she sighed, resigned to beginning once more.

"If it's anything to do with her, I was right to question you before disturbing my son. It is about her that you've come, isn't it?"

Did Maigret make a vague sign of assent? He was not aware of doing so. He was too intrigued by the atmosphere of this house, and even more by this woman, behind whose meekness he could sense an indomitable strength of will.

Everything about her was in good taste: her clothes, her

31

bearing, and her voice. She was someone you might meet in a château, or in one of those enormous country houses that are like museums of a bygone age.

"After my son became a widower, fifteen years ago, the thought of remarrying didn't enter his head for a long time."

"He did remarry, two years ago, if I'm not mistaken."

She showed no surprise at finding him so well informed.

"He did, indeed. Two and a half years ago exactly. He married one of his patients, a woman who was not young either. She was then forty-seven. Of Dutch origin, she lived alone in Paris. . . . I won't live forever, Chief Inspector. As you see me now, I am seventy-eight."

"You don't look it."

"I know. My mother lived to the age of ninety-two, and my grandmother was killed in an accident at ninety-eight."

"And your father?"

"He died young."

She spoke as though this was of no importance, or as if men in general were doomed to die young.

"I almost encouraged Guillaume to marry again, by saying that then he would not be left to live alone."

"The marriage was unhappy?"

"I wouldn't say that. Not to begin with. I think that the trouble arose mainly from her being a foreigner. There are all sorts of little things that one cannot get used to. I don't quite know how to explain. . . . Oh, yes. Food, for instance! A preference for this or that dish. Perhaps, too, when she married my son she imagined him to be wealthier than he actually is."

"She had no income of her own?"

"A certain amount. She was not badly off, but, with the rising cost of living . . ."

"When did she die?"

The old woman's eyes opened wide.

"Die?"

"I'm sorry. I thought she was dead. You speak of her in the past tense."

She smiled.

"That's true. But not for the reason you imagine. She isn't dead; but, for us, it's as though she were. She's gone away."

"After a quarrel?"

"Guillaume is not the kind of man who quarrels."

"With you?"

"I am too old to quarrel now, Chief Inspector. I've seen too much. I know life too well, and I let everybody—"

"When did she leave?"

"Two days ago."

"Did she tell you she was going?"

"My son and I knew that she would go, finally."

"She talked to you about it?"

"Often."

"Did she give you any reasons?"

She did not reply at once; she seemed to be pondering.

"Do you want me to tell you frankly what I think? If I hesitate, it's because I fear you may laugh at me. I don't like to discuss such things in front of men, but I suppose that a police inspector is rather like a doctor or a priest."

"You are a Roman Catholic, Madame Serre?"

"Yes. My daughter-in-law was a Protestant. . . . That

33

made no difference. You see, she was at an awkward age for a woman. We all, more or less, have to go through a few years during which we are not our normal selves. We get upset over trifles. We are apt to see things without perspective."

"I understand. That's what it was?"

"That, and other things, probably. She dreamed only of her native country, spent all day writing to friends she kept up with there."

"Did your son ever go to Holland with her?"

"Never."

"So she left on Tuesday?"

"She went on the nine-forty from Gare du Nord."

"The night train?"

"Yes. She had spent the whole day packing."

"Your son went with her to the station?"

"No."

"Did she take a taxi?"

"She went to get one at the corner of Boulevard Richard-Wallace."

"She hasn't been in touch with you since?"

"No. I don't suppose she feels it necessary to write to us."

"Was there any question of a divorce?"

"I've told you that we are Catholics. Moreover, my son has no wish to marry again. . . . I still do not understand why the police have seen fit to call upon us."

"I would like to ask you, madame, exactly what happened here on Tuesday night. . . . But first, you haven't a maid, have you?"

"No, Chief Inspector. We have a woman who comes every day from nine till five."

"Is she here today?"

"You have come on her day off. She'll be here again tomorrow."

"She lives in the neighborhood?"

"Eugénie lives in Puteaux, on the other side of the Seine. Above a hardware store directly opposite the bridge."

"I suppose she helped your daughter-in-law to pack?"

"She brought the luggage downstairs."

"How many pieces?"

"One trunk and two leather suitcases precisely. Then there was a jewel box and a cosmetics case."

"Eugénie left at five as usual?"

"She did indeed. . . . Please forgive me if I seem disconcerted, but this is the first time I've ever been questioned like this, and I must confess—"

"Did your son go out that evening?"

"What time of evening do you mean?"

"Let's say, before dinner."

"He went out for his usual stroll."

"I suppose he went to have an aperitif?"

"He doesn't drink."

"Never?"

"Nothing except a glass of wine-and-water at mealtimes. Never those horrible things called aperitifs."

Just then, Boissier, sitting in an armchair, on his best behavior, seemed to sniff the odor of aniseed that still clung to his mustache.

"We sat down to dinner as soon as he got back. He

35

always takes the same stroll. It became a habit with him in the days when we had a dog that had to be exercised at set times. Now, I declare, it's become second nature to him."

"You don't have a dog now?"

"Not for four years. Not since Bibi died."

"Or a cat?"

"My daughter-in-law loathed cats. . . . You see! I spoke of her again in the past tense, and it's because we really do think of her as belonging to the past."

"The three of you had dinner together?"

"Maria came down just as I was bringing in the soup."

"There was no quarreling?"

"None. Nobody spoke during the meal. I could tell that Guillaume, after all, was a little upset. At first, he seems cold, but really he's a terribly sensitive boy. When one has lived on terms of intimacy with someone for over two years . . ."

Maigret and Boissier had not heard a thing. But she, the old lady, was sharp of hearing. She bent her head as though she were listening. It was a mistake, because Maigret understood, rose to his feet, and went and opened the door. A man, undoubtedly taller, broader, and heavier than the Chief Inspector, stood there, slightly shamefaced; he had plainly been eavesdropping for some time.

His mother had told the truth when she claimed he was taking a siesta. His sparse hair, ruffled, clung to his forehead, and he'd pulled on a white shirt but left the top unbuttoned. He had carpet slippers on his feet.

"Won't you come in, Monsieur Serre?" asked Maigret.

"I beg your pardon. I heard voices. I thought . . ." He

36

spoke deliberately, turning his heavy, brooding stare upon each of them in turn.

"These gentlemen are police inspectors," his mother explained, rising to her feet.

He didn't ask for further explanation, merely stared at them again and buttoned his shirt.

"Madame Serre was telling us that your wife left the day before yesterday."

This time he turned to face the old lady, his brows drawn together. His big frame was flaccid, like his face, and, unlike some heavy men, he did not give an impression of agility. His complexion was very pale and sallow, tufts of dark hair sprouted from his nostrils, from his ears, and he had enormously bushy eyebrows.

"What exactly do these gentlemen want?" he finally asked, carefully spacing out the syllables.

"I don't know."

Even Maigret felt at a loss. Boissier wondered how the Chief was going to get out of the situation. These weren't the sort of people you could put through the third degree.

"Actually, Monsieur Serre, the question of your wife merely cropped up in the course of conversation. Your mother told us that you were lying down, and we had a little talk while we were waiting for you. We are here, my colleague and I"—the term "colleague" gave Boissier so much pleasure!—"simply because we have reason to believe that you have been the victim of an attempted burglary."

Serre was not a man unable to look others in the face. Far from it. He stared at Maigret as though attempting to read his innermost thoughts.

"What gave you that idea?"

37

"Sometimes we come into possession of confidential information."

"You are speaking, I suppose, of police informers?"

"Let's put it like that."

"I'm sorry, gentlemen."

"Your house hasn't been robbed?"

"If it had been, I would have lost no time in lodging a complaint myself with the local police."

He wasn't trying to be civil. Not once had he shown even the vestige of a smile.

"You are the owner of a safe?"

"I believe that I'd be within my rights in refusing to answer you. I don't mind telling you, however, that I do have one."

His mother was making signs to him, advising him, seemingly, not to be so ill-tempered.

He realized this but remained obdurate.

"If I'm not mistaken, it's a safe installed by Planchart about eighteen years ago."

Unperturbed, he continued to stand, while Maigret and Boissier sat in the semidarkness. Maigret saw that he had the same heavy jowl as the man in the portrait, the same eyebrows. The Chief Inspector wondered whimsically what he'd look like with side whiskers.

"I don't remember when I had it put in. Nor is that anybody's business but mine."

"I noticed, as we came in, that the front door is secured by a chain and a safety lock."

"So are lots of front doors."

"You sleep on the second floor, your mother and you?"

Serre deliberately made no reply.

"Your study and dental office are on the ground floor?"

From a gesture on the part of the old lady, Maigret understood that those rooms led out of the drawing room.

"Would you mind if I take a look around?"

Serre opened his mouth, and Maigret felt certain it was to say no. His mother sensed this, too, and intervened.

"Why not comply with these gentlemen's request? They will see for themselves that there has been no burglary."

The man shrugged, his expression as stubborn, as sullen, as ever. He did not follow them into the adjoining rooms.

Madame Serre showed them first into a study as peaceful and old-fashioned as the drawing room. Behind a black leather chair stood a big safe, painted dark green, of a rather obsolete type. Boissier went up to it and stroked the steel with a professional touch.

"You see that everything is in order," said the old woman. "You mustn't mind my son's being in a bad temper, but . . ."

She stopped as she saw him, framed in the doorway, fixing them with the same morose stare.

Waving a hand toward the bound volumes that filled the shelves, she went on, with strained sprightliness.

"Don't be surprised to see they are mostly books on law. They're part of the library that belonged to my husband, who was a lawyer."

She opened another door. Here the furnishings were more ordinary; it might have been any dental office, with a mechanical chair and the usual instruments. Up to half the height of the windows, the panes were frosted.

On their way back through the study Boissier crossed to one of the windows, ran his fingers over it, then gave Maigret a significant nod.

"Has this windowpane been put in recently?" asked the latter.

It was the old woman who answered, immediately.

"Four or five days ago. The window was broken during the big thunderstorm, which I'm sure you remember."

"Did you call in the glazier?"

"No."

"Who replaced the pane?"

"My son. He likes doing odd jobs. He always sees to any of our little household repairs."

At this, Guillaume Serre said, with a touch of irritation: "These gentleman have no right to pester us, Mama. Don't answer any more questions."

She turned so her back was toward him, and smiled at Maigret in a way that meant plainly: "Don't mind him. I did warn you."

She showed them to the front door, while her son remained standing in the center of the drawing room, and she leaned forward to whisper: "If you have anything to say to me, come and call when he isn't here."

They were outside in the sunlight again, and the heat made their shirts cling to their skin. Once beyond the gate—its faint creak reminiscent of a convent gate—they caught sight of Ernestine's green hat as she sat at a table outside the bistro on the opposite side of the street.

Maigret stopped. They could have turned left and avoided her. If they joined her, it would look almost as though they had to give her an account of what they'd found out.

Perhaps out of a sense of propriety, the Chief Inspector growled: "Shall we go and have one?"

With an inquiring expression, she watched them come toward her.

3

"What did you do today?" asked Madame Maigret as they sat down to eat by the open window.

In the houses opposite also, people could be seen eating, with the same white splashes showing that the men had taken off their jackets. Some of those who had finished dinner were leaning on their elbows at the window. Radio music could be heard, as well as crying babies and raised voices. A few concierges had taken their chairs out to sit on their doorsteps.

"Nothing out of the way," replied Maigret. "A Dutchwoman who may have been murdered, but who may, instead, be still alive somewhere."

It was too early to talk about it. On the whole, he'd

shown slackness. They'd sat for a long time outside the little bistro on rue de la Ferme—Boissier, Ernestine, and himself—and of the three it was Ernestine who'd reacted the most. She'd taken umbrage.

"He made out it wasn't true?"

The proprietor had brought them glasses of beer.

"Actually, he didn't say anything. It was his mother who did the talking. Alone, he'd have thrown us out."

"He says there wasn't a corpse in the study?"

She'd obviously found out from the proprietor about the residents of the house with the wrought-iron gate.

"Why didn't he tell the police that somebody tried to burgle the place?"

"According to him, no one tried to rob him."

Of course she knew all about Sad Freddie's little ways.

"Wasn't there a pane missing in one of the windows?" she asked.

Boissier looked at Maigret as if advising him to say nothing, but the Chief Inspector took no notice.

"A pane has been replaced recently. It seems that it got broken four or five days ago, on the night of the storm."

"They're lying."

"Somebody's lying, certainly."

"You think it's me?"

"I didn't say so. It might be Alfred."

"Why should he have told me that story on the phone?"

"Perhaps he didn't," interposed Boissier, watching her narrowly.

"What would I have made it up for? . . . Is that what you think, too, Monsieur Maigret?"

"I don't think anything."

43

He was smiling vaguely. He felt comfortable, almost bliss-ful. The beer was cool, and in the shade it smelled almost like the country, perhaps because the Bois de Boulogne was close by.

A lazy afternoon. They'd drunk two glasses apiece. Then, in order not to leave the girl stranded so far from the center of Paris, they gave her a lift in their taxi, dropping her at the Châtelet Métro stop.

"Call me as soon as you get a letter."

He felt she was disappointed in him, that he wasn't what she'd imagined. She must be thinking that he'd got old, had become like the rest of them, and couldn't really be bothered with her problem.

"Do you want me to put off my vacation?" Boissier had asked.

"I suppose your wife's done all the packing?"

"The bags are at the station already. We're due to go on the six o'clock train tomorrow morning."

"With your daughter?"

"Naturally."

"Off you go."

"Won't you be needing me?"

"You've trusted me with the file."

Once alone in his office, Maigret nearly dozed off in his chair. The wasp was no longer there, and the sun had moved around to the other side of the quay.

Lucas had been off duty since noon. So Maigret called in Janvier, who'd been the first to take his vacation, back in June, for a wedding in some branch of his family.

"Sit down. I have a job for you. You've got your report done?"

"I've just this minute finished it."

"Good. First, I want you to look up, in Neuilly, the maiden name of a Dutchwoman who, two and a half years ago, married a man named Guillaume Serre, residing at 43b, rue de la Ferme."

"Easy."

"Probably. She must have been living in Paris for some time. Try to find out where, what she did, what relatives she had, how much money, and so on . . ."

"All right."

"She's supposed to have left the house on rue de la Ferme on Tuesday, between eight and nine in the evening, and to have taken the night train to Holland. She went to get a taxi at the corner of Boulevard Richard-Wallace, to take her luggage."

Janvier was writing in columns on a page of his notebook.

"That all?"

"No. Get some help, to save time. I want the people in the neighborhood, shopkeepers and so on, questioned about the Serres."

"How many are there?"

"Mother and son. The mother's nearly eighty, and the son's a dentist. Try to locate the taxi. Also make inquiries at the station and with the train crew."

"Can I have a car?"

"You can."

That was about all he'd done that afternoon, though he'd called the Belgian police, who had Sad Freddie's description but had not yet found him. He also had a long conversation with the border passport inspectors at Jeumont. The one who had checked the train Alfred was thought to have taken didn't remember any passenger resembling the expert safecracker.

That meant nothing. He simply had to wait. He signed a few papers on behalf of the Big Chief, went to have a drink at the Brasserie Dauphine with a colleague from the Records Office, and then rode home by bus.

"What shall we do?" asked Madame Maigret when the table had been cleared.

"Let's go for a walk."

This meant they'd amble along as far as the Grands Boulevards, and then sit on a café terrace. The sun had set. It was getting cooler, though gusts of warm air still seemed to rise from the sidewalk. The windows of the brasserie were open, and a depleted orchestra was playing inside. Most of the customers sat without talking, just as they, at their table, did, watching the passers-by. Their faces gradually melted into the dusk. Soon the streetlight made them look quite different.

Like other couples, they turned toward home, Madame Maigret's hand tucked in her husband's arm.

After that, it was another day, as clear and sunny as the one before.

Instead of going straight to the Police Judiciaire, Maigret made a detour by Quai de Jemmapes, found the green-painted café, near the St. Martin lock, with the sign SNACKS SERVED AT ALL HOURS, and went in. Leaning against the zinc counter, he said: "A white wine." Then he put the question.

The Auvergnat who served him answered without hesitating. "I don't know what time exactly, but someone called. It was toward daylight. My wife and I didn't get up, because, at that time, it couldn't have been for us. Ernestine went down. I heard her talking a long time."

That was one thing, at least, she had not lied about.

"What time did Alfred go out, the night before?"

"Eleven, maybe? Maybe earlier. What I do remember is that he took his bike."

A door led straight from the café into the hallway, from which stairs led to the floors above. The wall of the staircase was whitewashed, as in the country. The racket made by a crane unloading gravel from a barge a little farther on could be heard.

Maigret knocked at a door, which half opened. Ernestine stood there in her underclothes and merely said: "It's you!"

Then she went at once to get her dressing gown from the unmade bed and slipped it on.

Did Maigret smile in memory of the Ernestine-that-used-to-be?

"You know, it's really a kindness," she said frankly. "I'm not a pretty sight these days."

The window was open. There was a blood-red geranium on the sill. The bedspread was red, too. The door to a little kitchen stood open; from it came a smell of good coffee.

He didn't quite know why he was there.

"Nothing at poste restante last evening?"

She answered, looking worried: "Nothing."

47

"Don't you think it odd he hasn't written?"

"Maybe he's just being cagey. He must be surprised to see nothing in the papers. He probably thinks I'm being watched. . . . I was just going to the post office."

An old trunk lay in a corner.

"Those are his belongings?"

"His and mine. Between the two of us, we don't own much."

Then, with an understanding look: "Like to make a search? I know it's your duty. You'll find a few tools, because he has a spare set. Also two old suits, some dresses, and some underwear."

As she spoke, she took out the contents of the trunk, put them on the floor, and opened the drawers of a dressing table.

"I've been thinking it over. I see what you were getting at yesterday. Of course somebody must be lying. Either it's those people, the mother and son, or it's Alfred, or it's me. You have no reason to believe any of us in particular."

"Has Alfred any relatives in the country?"

"He has no relatives anywhere now. He knew only his mother, and she's been dead twenty years."

"You've never been anywhere together outside Paris?"

"Never farther than Corbeil."

He couldn't be hiding out in Corbeil. It was too near. Maigret was beginning to think that he hadn't gone to Belgium, either.

"There's no place he talked about, that he'd like to visit someday?"

"He always said 'the country,' no special part. That summed it all up for him."

48

"Were you born in the country?"

"Near Nevers, in a village called St.-Martin-des-Près."

She took from a drawer a postcard that showed the village church, standing opposite a pond used to water cattle.

"Did you show him this?"

She understood. Girls like Ernestine understood quickly.

"I'd be surprised to find him there. He really was near Gare du Nord when he phoned me."

"How do you know?"

"I found the bistro last evening. It's on rue de Maubeuge, near a leather-goods shop. It's called the Levant. . . . The owner remembers him because he was the first customer that day. He'd just put on the coffee when Alfred came in. . . . Would you like a cup of coffee?"

He didn't like to refuse, but he'd just drunk white wine.

"No offense."

After some difficulty finding a taxi, Maigret rode to the Levant.

"A thin little guy, sad-looking. His eyes were all red, as if he'd been crying," he was told.

Unquestionably it was Alfred Jussiaume, who often had red-rimmed eyes.

"He talked a long time on the phone, drank two coffees, without sugar, and then went off toward the station, looking around as if he was scared of being followed. . . . Has he done something wrong?"

It was ten o'clock when Maigret at last climbed the stairs at the PJ, where dust motes floated like a mist in the sunlight. Contrary to his usual custom, he didn't glance through the glass windows of the waiting room, but went straight to the duty room, which was almost empty.

49

"Janvier not in yet?"

"He came about eight and went out again. He left a note on your desk."

The note said:

The woman is Maria Van Aerts. Fifty-one. Comes from Sneeck, in Friesland. I'm going to Neuilly, where she lived in a boardinghouse, rue de Longchamp. Haven't found taxi yet. Vacher's taking care of station.

Joseph opened the door.

"I didn't see you come in, Monsieur Maigret. A lady's been waiting for you half an hour."

He held out a slip, on which old Madame Serre had inscribed her name in small, pointed handwriting.

"Shall I show her in?"

Maigret put on the jacket he'd just taken off, went to open the window, filled his pipe, and sat down.

"Yes, show her in."

He wondered what she would seem like outside the framework of her home. To his surprise, she didn't look out of place at all. She wasn't dressed in black, as on the day before; she wore a dress with a white background, on which dark patterns were traced. Her hat was not ludicrous. She moved forward with assurance.

"You were more or less expecting me to call, weren't you, Chief Inspector?"

He had not been expecting it, but refrained from telling her so.

"Do sit down, madame."

"Thank you."

50

"The smoke doesn't bother you?"

"My son smokes cigars all day long. . . . I was so upset yesterday by the way he received you! I tried to signal you not to persist, because I know him."

She showed no nervousness, chose her words carefully, and aimed at Maigret now and then a sort of conspiratorial smile.

"I think it is I who brought him up badly. You see, I had only the one child, and when my husband died, my son was seventeen years old. I spoiled him. . . . Guillaume was the only man in the house. If you have children . . ."

Maigret was trying to guess her background, without success. Something made him ask: "Were you born in Paris?"

"In the house you came to yesterday."

It was a coincidence to find in one case two people born in Paris. Almost invariably the people he dealt with were connected more or less with the provinces.

"And your husband?"

"His father, before him, used to be a lawyer on rue de Tocqueville, in the Seventeenth Arrondissement."

That made three! And they ended up in an atmosphere so absolutely provincial, on rue de la Ferme!

"My son and I have almost always lived alone together, and I suppose that is what has made him a little unsociable."

"You said he'd been married before?"

"He was. His wife didn't live long."

"How many years after their marriage did she die?"

She opened her mouth; he guessed that a sudden thought made her pause. He even thought he saw a slight flush mount to her cheeks.

"Two years," she said at last. "That's curious, is it not?

51

It only struck me now. He lived for two years with Maria, as well."

"Who was his first wife?"

"A person of very good family, Jeanne Devoisin, whom we met one summer in Dieppe. We used to go there every year."

"Was she younger than he?"

"Let me see. . . . He was thirty-two. She was more or less the same age. She was a widow."

"Any children?"

"No. I don't think she had any relatives except a sister living in Indochina."

"What did she die of?"

"A heart attack. She had a weak heart and spent most of her time under the care of doctors."

She smiled again.

"I haven't told you yet why I am here. . . . I nearly telephoned you yesterday, when my son went out for his stroll. But I thought it would be more polite to come and call on you. I wish to apologize for Guillaume's attitude toward you and to say that his ill humor was not directed at you personally. He has such a hostile temperament."

"So I saw."

"At the very idea that you could suspect him of doing something dishonest . . . He was like that even as a small boy. . . ."

"He lied to me."

"I beg your pardon?"

The old lady's face expressed genuine surprise.

"Why should he have lied to you? I don't understand. You didn't really ask any questions. . . . It's precisely to

52

answer any you wish to put to me that I have come here. We have nothing to hide. I do not know the circumstances that led you to bother about us. It must be owing to some misunderstanding, or some neighbor's spitefulness."

"When was the windowpane broken?"

"I told you—or my son told you; I can't remember now—during the thunderstorm last week. I was upstairs, and I hadn't had time to shut all the windows when I heard a crash of glass."

"Was it in broad daylight?"

"It must have been six o'clock in the evening."

"Which means Eugénie was no longer there?"

"She leaves us at five; I think I explained that to you also. . . . I didn't tell my son that I was coming to see you. I thought that you might like, perhaps, to visit the house, and it would be easier when he's not there."

"You mean during his late afternoon stroll?"

"Yes. You do understand that there's nothing to hide in our home, and that if it weren't for Guillaume's nature, everything would have been cleared up yesterday."

"You realize, Madame Serre, that you came here of your own free will?"

"Yes, of course."

"And that it's you who want me to question you?"

She nodded her head in confirmation.

"We'll go over your movements again, then, from the last meal that you, your son, and your daughter-in-law took together. Your daughter-in-law's luggage was ready. Where was it?"

"In the entrance hallway."

"Who brought it down?"

53

"Eugénie brought down the suitcases, and my son took charge of the trunk, which was too heavy for her."

"Is it a very big trunk?"

"What they call a wardrobe trunk. Before her marriage, Maria traveled a lot. She has lived in Italy and Egypt."

"What did you have to eat?"

The question seemed both to amuse her and surprise her.

"Let me see! Since I do the cooking, I should be able to remember. . . . Vegetable soup, to start with. We always have vegetable soup; it's so good for the health. Then we had grilled mackerel and potato purée."

"And the dessert?"

"Chocolate custard. My son has always adored chocolate custard."

"No argument broke out at the table? . . . What time did the meal end?"

"About half past seven. I put the dishes in the kitchen sink and went upstairs."

"So you weren't present at the departure of your daughter-in-law."

"I wasn't very anxious to be there. Moments such as those are painful, and I prefer to avoid emotion. I said au revoir to her downstairs, in the drawing room. . . . I have nothing against her. People are as they are made and—"

"Where was your son during that time?"

"In his study, I think."

"Do you know whether he had a last conversation with his wife?"

"It's unlikely. She'd gone upstairs again. I heard her in her room, getting ready."

"Your house is very solidly built, like most old houses. I

suppose that on the second floor it's hard to hear sounds downstairs?"

"Not for me," she answered, pursing her lips.

"What do you mean?"

"That I have keen hearing. Not even a floorboard can creak without my hearing it."

"Who went to get the taxi?"

"Maria. I told you so yesterday."

"Was she gone long?"

"Fairly long. There's no stand nearby, and one has to wait for a taxi to come cruising by."

"Did you go to the window?"

She hesitated imperceptibly.

"Yes."

"Who carried the trunk to the taxi?"

"The driver."

"What company did he belong to?"

"How would I know that?"

"What color was the taxi?"

"Reddish brown, with a symbol on the door."

"Can you remember the driver?"

"Not very well. I think he was small and rather fat."

"How was your daughter-in-law dressed?"

"She wore a mauve dress."

"No coat?"

"She had it over her arm."

"Was your son still in the study?"

"Yes."

"What happened then? Did you go down?"

"No."

"You didn't go to see your son?"

55

"He came up."

"Immediately?"

"Not long after the taxi drove away."

"Was he upset?"

"He was as you saw him. He has a rather gloomy nature. I explained to you that he's really highly sensitive, and likely to be affected even by the smallest happenings."

"Did he know that his wife was not coming back?"

"He suspected it."

"She told him so?"

"Not exactly. She just hinted. She talked about how she needed to change her ideas, to see her own country again. Once there, you understand—"

"What did you do then?"

"I fixed my hair for the night."

"Your son was in the room?"

"Yes."

"He didn't leave the house?"

"No. . . . Why?"

"Where does he keep his car?"

"A hundred yards away. Some old stables have been turned into private garages. Guillaume rents one of them."

"So he can take his car out and put it back in without being seen?"

"Why should he want to hide?"

"Did he go downstairs again?"

"I don't remember. I think so. I go to bed early, and he usually reads until eleven o'clock or midnight."

"In the study?"

"Or in his room."

"His room is near yours?"

56

"Next door. There's a bathroom between us."

"Did you hear him go to bed?"

"Certainly."

"When?"

"I didn't put on the light."

"You didn't hear any noise later?"

"None."

"I suppose that you're the first one down in the morning?"

"In summer I go down at half past six."

"Did you go into all the rooms?"

"I went first to the kitchen, to put water on to boil. Then I opened the windows, because that's when the air is still cool."

"You went into the study, too?"

"Probably."

"You don't remember doing so?"

"I almost certainly did."

"The broken pane was already repaired?"

"I suppose so. . . . Yes . . ."

"Did you notice any thing out of order in the room?"

"No, except for some cigar butts, as always, in the ashtrays. Maybe a book or two lying around . . . I don't know what all this means, Monsieur Maigret. As you see, I answer your questions frankly. I came especially to do so."

"Because you're worried?"

"No. Because I was ashamed of the way Guillaume treated you. And also because I sense something mysterious behind your visit. Women aren't like men. In my husband's time, for instance, if there was a noise in the house at night, he never moved from his bed; it was I who went to look. You understand? It's probably the same with your own wife.

57

. . . Really, it is, in a way, for the same reason that I'm here. You talked about burglary. You seemed preoccupied with the question of Maria."

"You haven't had any news of her?"

"I don't expect to receive any. . . . You're hiding certain facts, and that makes me curious. It is the same with sounds in the night. I hold that mysteries don't exist, that one has only to look at things squarely for them to become perfectly simple."

She was watching him, sure of herself, and Maigret had a slight feeling that she looked upon him as a child, as another Guillaume. She seemed to be saying:

"Tell me everything that's worrying you. Don't be frightened. You'll see that it'll come out all right."

He looked her straight in the face.

"A man broke into your house that night."

The old woman's eyes were incredulous, with a tinge of pity, as though he still believed in werewolves.

"What for?"

"To rob the safe."

"Did he do it?"

"He got into the house by cutting out a pane of glass to open the window."

"The pane that was broken in the thunderstorm? Well, no doubt he put it back afterward."

She refused to take what he was saying seriously.

"What did he take?"

"He took nothing, because at a certain moment his flashlight showed him something he hadn't expected to find there."

She was smiling.

"What sort of thing?"

"The dead body of a middle-aged woman, which may have been that of your daughter-in-law."

"He told you that?"

He looked at the white-gloved hands; they weren't trembling.

"Why don't you ask this man to come and repeat his accusations to me?" she asked.

"He's not in Paris."

"Can't you make him come here?"

Maigret preferred not to reply. He wasn't too pleased with himself. He was beginning to wonder if he, too, was not falling under the influence of this woman, who had the comforting serenity of a mother superior.

She didn't get up, didn't fidget, didn't show indignation, either.

"I have no idea what it's all about, and I won't ask you. Perhaps you have some good reason for believing this man. He's a burglar, isn't he? While I am merely an old woman of seventy-eight who never did anyone any harm.

"Allow me, now that I know where we stand, to invite you cordially to come to our house. I will open every door for you. I will show you anything you may wish to see. And my son, once he is acquainted with the facts, will not fail, in his turn, to answer your questions.

"When will you come, Monsieur Maigret?"

Now she had risen to her feet, but was still perfectly at ease. There was nothing aggressive in her manner, just a slight touch of bitterness.

"Probably this afternoon. I don't know yet. . . . Has your son used the car these last few days?"

59

"You can ask him, if you like."

"Is he at home now?"

"It's possible. He was there when I left."

"Eugénie, too?"

"She is certainly there."

"Thank you."

He showed her to the door. Just as they reached it, she turned around.

"I'd like to ask a favor," she said gently. "When I've gone, try for a moment to put yourself in my place, forgetting that you have spent your life dealing with crime. Imagine that it's you who are suddenly being asked the questions you put to me, you who are being suspected of killing someone in cold blood."

That was all. She only added: "Until this afternoon, Monsieur Maigret."

Once the door was closed, he stood by it for a full minute without moving. Then he went to look out the window. He soon caught sight of the old lady, walking with quick short steps, in full sunshine, toward Pont St.-Michel.

He picked up the telephone.

"Get me the police in Neuilly."

He didn't ask for the Superintendent, but for an inspector he knew.

"Vanneau? Maigret. . . . I'm well, thanks. Listen. It's a little tricky. Jump in a car and go around to 43b, rue de la Ferme."

"The dentist's place? Janvier, who was here last night, told me about him. Something to do with a Dutchwoman, isn't it?"

"Never mind. Time's passing. The fellow's not easy to

60

handle, and I can't ask for a warrant yet. You've got to act quickly, before his mother gets there."

"Is she far away?"

"At Pont St.-Michel. She's probably going to take a taxi."

"What shall I do with the man?"

"Take him in, on some excuse. Tell him whatever you like, that you need him as a witness . . ."

"And then?"

"I'll be there. In the time it takes to get downstairs and into a car."

"Suppose he's not home?"

"Keep watch and grab him before he gets inside."

"A little irregular, isn't it?"

"Very."

As Vanneau was about to hang up, Maigret added: "Take somebody with you, and get him to watch the stables they've turned into garages, on the same street. One of them is rented by the dentist."

"I've got it."

A moment later Maigret was hurrying down the stairs and getting into one of the police cars parked in the court- yard. As it turned toward Pont Neuf, he thought he caught sight of Ernestine's green hat. He wasn't sure, though, and preferred not to lose time. To tell the truth, he was suddenly feeling resentment toward Lofty.

Once they'd crossed Pont Neuf, he felt remorseful, but it was too late.

Couldn't be helped! She'd wait for him.

4

The police commissariat was on the ground floor of an ugly square building that stood in the middle of a wasteland with a few trees and a dirty flag dangling from a pole. Maigret could have gone straight to the duty room, but in order not to come face to face with Guillaume Serre, he took a round-about way through drafty corridors, where he soon got lost.

Here, too, the slackness of summer held sway. Doors and windows were open, documents fluttered on tables in empty rooms, clerks in shirtsleeves exchanged vacation tales, and an occasional taxpayer wandered disconsolately in search of an endorsement or a signature.

Maigret finally managed to light upon a policeman who knew him by sight.

"Inspector Vanneau?"

"Second corridor on the left, third door along."

"Would you go and get him for me. There should be someone with him. Don't say my name out loud."

A few moments later Vanneau joined him.

"Is he there?"

"Yes."

"How did it go?"

"So-so. I rang, a servant answered, and I asked to see her master. I had to wait around a while in the hall. Then the fellow came downstairs, and I handed him the summons I'd made sure to take. He read it and looked at me without saying anything.

" 'If you'd come with me, I have a car outside.'

"He shrugged, took a Panama hat from the hall stand, shoved it on his head, and followed me out.

"Now he's sitting on a chair. . . . He hasn't said a word."

A minute or two later Maigret went into Vanneau's office and found Serre there smoking a very black cigar. The Chief Inspector sat in Vanneau's chair.

"I'm sorry to trouble you, Monsieur Serre, but I'd like you to answer a few questions."

As he had the day before, the huge dentist surveyed him broodingly, with no trace of cordiality in his gloomy stare. Maigret, all of a sudden, realized what the man reminded him of: the sort of sultan one used to see in illustrations. He had the girth, the manifest weight; in all probability, the strength, too; despite his fat, he gave the impression of being very strong. And he had the disdainful calm of the pashas depicted on cigarette packages.

Instead of making some sign of agreement, uttering a

63

polite commonplace, or voicing a protest, Serre took a buff-colored form from his pocket and cast his eye over it.

"I've been summoned here by the Police Superintendent of Neuilly," he said. "I look forward to hearing what this superintendent requires of me."

"Am I to understand you refuse to answer my questions?"

"Emphatically."

Maigret paused. He'd seen all kinds, the mutinous, the pigheaded, the willful, the wily, but none had ever answered him back with such unruffled determination.

"I suppose it's no good arguing?"

"Not in my opinion."

"Or trying to point out that your attitude doesn't show you in a good light?"

This time the other merely sighed.

"Very well. Wait."

Maigret went in search of the Superintendent, who did not understand right away what was expected of him, and only grudgingly agreed to play his part. His quarters were more comfortable, almost sumptuous in comparison with the rest of the offices. There was even a marble clock on the mantelpiece.

"Show Monsieur Serre in!" he told the man on duty.

He motioned him to a chair with a red velvet seat.

"Do sit down, Monsieur Serre. It's just a matter of a routine check, and I won't waste your time."

The Superintendent consulted a form that had just been brought to him.

"You are, I believe, the owner of a motor vehicle registered under the number RS8822L?"

The dentist confirmed this with a nod. Maigret had gone over to sit on the windowsill and was watching him very thoughtfully.

"The vehicle in question is still in your possession?"

Another nod of assent.

"When was the last time you used it?"

"I believe I have the right to know the reason for this interrogation."

The Superintendent shifted in his chair. He didn't at all like the task Maigret had given him.

"Suppose that your car was involved in some accident . . ."

"Has it been?"

"Suppose the number was given to us as that of a car that had knocked somebody down."

"When?"

The Superintendent threw Maigret a reproachful look.

"Tuesday evening."

"Where?"

"Near the Seine."

"My car didn't leave the garage on Tuesday evening."

"Somebody might have used it without your knowledge."

"I doubt it. The garage is locked."

"You're prepared to swear that you didn't use the car on Tuesday evening, or later during that night?"

"Where are the witnesses to this accident?"

Once again the Superintendent looked anxiously to Maigret for support. The latter, realizing that this was leading nowhere, motioned to him not to take it any further.

"I have no more questions, Monsieur Serre. Thank you."

65

The dentist rose, seeming for a moment to fill the room with his bulk, put on his Panama hat, and left the room after turning to glare at Maigret.

"I did what I could. As you saw."

"I saw."

"Did you get a lead out of it?"

"Maybe."

"That's a man who'll make trouble for us. He's a stickler for his rights."

"I know."

It seemed almost as if Maigret was unconsciously imitating the dentist. He had the same somber, heavy expression. He, in turn, made for the door.

"What's he supposed to have done, Maigret?"

"I don't know yet. It may be that he killed his wife."

He went to thank Vanneau. Outside once more, he found the police car waiting for him, but before getting in he had a drink at the bistro on the corner. Catching sight of himself in the mirror over the counter, he wondered what he'd look like wearing a Panama hat. Then he smiled wryly at the thought that it was, in a way, a case of two heavyweights engaged in a fight.

He said to the driver: "Go around by rue de la Ferme."

Not far from 43b they caught sight of Serre, walking along rather indolently. As some fat men do, he straddled slightly. He was still smoking his big cigar. As he passed the garage, he couldn't have failed to notice the inspector keeping a lookout there, who had no means of taking cover.

Maigret was reluctant to stop at the house with the black

wrought-iron gate. What good would it do? They probably wouldn't let him in.

Ernestine was waiting for him in the glass-paneled waiting room at the PJ. He showed her into his office.

"Any news?" she asked him.

"Not a thing."

He was in a bad mood. She didn't know that he rather liked feeling bad-tempered in the early days of a difficult case.

"I had a card this morning. I've brought it to you."

She handed him a colored postcard of the town hall at Le Havre. There was no message, no signature, nothing but Lofty's name and Poste Restante, Paris.

"Alfred?"

"It's his handwriting."

"He didn't go to Belgium?"

"Doesn't look like it. He must have steered clear of the border."

"Do you think he might try to get away by sea?"

"Not likely. He's never set foot on a boat. . . . I'm going to ask you something, Monsieur Maigret, but you've got to give me a straight answer. Suppose he was to come back to Paris: What would happen to him?"

"You want to know if he'd be held in custody?"

"Yes."

"For attempted burglary?"

"Yes."

"Nobody could detain him, because he wasn't caught red-handed. For another thing, Guillaume Serre hasn't filed a complaint, even denies that anybody broke into his house."

"So they'd let him alone?"

"Unless he was lying and something quite different happened."

"Can I promise him that?"

"Yes."

"In that case, I'll put a notice in the personals column. He always takes the same paper, because of the crossword puzzle."

She looked at him hard for a moment.

"You don't seem too sure about things."

"What things?"

"The case. Yourself . . . I don't know . . . Did you see the dentist again?"

"Half an hour ago."

"What did he say?"

"Nothing."

She had nothing more to say, either, and used the telephone's ringing as an excuse to leave.

"What is it?" Maigret growled into the mouthpiece.

"It's me, Chief. Can I see you in your office?"

A few seconds later Janvier came in briskly, obviously very pleased with himself.

"I've got plenty of leads. Shall I give them to you right away? You have a little time to spare?"

His enthusiasm was somewhat damped by Maigret's behavior. The Chief just taken off his coat and was loosening his tie to set his thick neck free.

"First, I went to the boardinghouse I told you about. It's a little like the hotels on the Left Bank, with potted palms in the lobby and old ladies sitting around in wicker chairs. There aren't many guests much under fifty. Most of them

68

are foreigners—Englishwomen, Swiss, Americans—who go to museums and write endless letters."

"Well?"

Maigret knew the kind of thing. It wasn't worth going on about it.

"Maria Van Aerts lived there for a year. They remember her because she made herself popular in the place. She seems to have been very happy and laughed a lot, shaking a great big bosom. She used to stuff herself with pastries, and went to lots of lectures at the Sorbonne."

"That all?" said Maigret, meaning that he couldn't see what Janvier was so pleased about.

"Nearly every day she wrote letters, eight or ten pages."

The Chief Inspector shrugged his shoulders, but then looked at the Inspector with more interest in his eyes. He had caught on.

"Always to the same woman, a school friend who lives in Amsterdam and whose name I have. This friend came to see her once. They shared a room for three weeks. I think that even after she married, Maria Serre kept on writing to her. The friend is Gertrude Oosting; she's the wife of a brewer. It shouldn't be hard to find out her address."

"Call Amsterdam."

"Will you want the letters?"

"The recent ones, if possible."

"That's what I thought. . . . Brussels still hasn't any news of Sad Freddie."

"He's in Le Havre."

"Shall I call there?"

"I'll do it myself. Who's free next door?"

"Torrence came back on duty this morning."

"Send him in."

He was another heavyweight, and wouldn't pass unnoticed on the sidewalk of an empty street.

"Go and stick yourself down in Neuilly, rue de la Ferme, facing 43b, a house with a garden and an iron gate in front. Don't bother to hide. Far from it. If you see a man come out, bigger and taller than you, follow him so he can see you."

"Anything else?"

"Arrange to be relieved part of the night. There's a man from Neuilly on duty farther along, opposite the garage."

"What if the fellow goes off by car?"

"Take one of ours and park it by the curb."

He didn't have the energy to go home for lunch. It was hotter than the day before. There was thunder in the air. Most men were walking with their jackets over their arms, and urchins were swimming in the Seine.

He went to have a bite at the Brasserie Dauphine, first drinking, as if as a challenge, a couple of Pernods. Then he went to see Moers, of the Forensic Lab, beneath the overheated roof of the Palais de Justice.

"Let's say about eleven. Bring the necessary gear, and someone else."

"Yes, Chief."

He had called the police in Le Havre. Had Sad Freddie really taken a train at Gare du Nord, but to Lille, for instance? Or, after he'd telephoned Ernestine, had he made a dash for Gare St.-Lazare?

He might have gone to some cheap room, or wandered from bistro to bistro, drinking small bottles of Vichy water,

70

unless he was trying to stow away on board some ship. Was it as hot in Le Havre as it was in Paris?

They still hadn't found the taxi that was supposed to have picked up Maria Serre and her luggage. The employees at Gare du Nord had no recollection of her.

Opening the paper, about three o'clock, Maigret read Ernestine's message in the personals column:

ALFRED. RETURN PARIS. NO DANGER.
ALL ARRANGED. TINE.

At half past four he found himself still in his chair, the newspaper on his knees. He hadn't turned the page. He'd gone to sleep, and his mouth felt sticky, his back cricked.

None of the cars was in the courtyard, so he had to take a taxi from the end of the quay.

"Rue de la Ferme, in Neuilly. I'll show you where to stop."

He nearly dozed off again. It was five to five when he stopped the taxi opposite the now familiar bistro. There was no one at the tables outside. Farther on, the burly shape of Torrence could be seen, pacing up and down in the shade. He paid the driver and sat down with a sigh of relief.

"What can I get you, Monsieur Maigret?"

Beer, of course! He was so thirsty he could have swallowed five or six glasses at a gulp.

"Has he been in again?"

"The dentist? No . . . I saw his mother, this morning, going down toward Boulevard Richard-Wallace."

The wrought-iron gate creaked. A wiry little woman started to walk along the opposite sidewalk. Maigret, settled

71

for his drink, caught up to her just as she reached the edge of the Bois de Boulogne.

"Madame Eugénie?"

"What do you want?"

The Neuilly household wasn't conspicuous for its affability.

"A little chat with you."

"I don't have time to chat. There's all the housework to do when I get home."

"I'm from the police."

"That makes no difference."

"I'd like to ask you a few questions."

"Do I have to answer?"

"It would certainly be better to."

"I don't like policemen."

"You're not obliged to. Do you like your employers?"

"They're horrible."

"Old Madame Serre, too?"

"She's a bitch."

They were standing by a bus stop. Maigret raised his arm to stop a cruising taxi.

"I'll take you home."

"I don't like it much to be seen with a cop, but I suppose it's worth it."

She got in the taxi with dignity.

"What have you got against them?"

"What about you? Why are you sticking your nose into their business?"

"Young Madame Serre has gone away?"

"Young?" she said ironically.

"Let's say, the daughter-in-law."

72

"She's gone, yes. Good riddance."

"Was she a bitch, too?"

"No."

"But you didn't like her?"

"She was always digging into the larder, and when lunchtime came, I couldn't find half what I'd got ready."

"When did she go?"

"Tuesday."

They were crossing Pont de Puteaux. Eugénie tapped on the glass.

"Here we are," she said. "Do you need me any more?"

"Could I come up with you for a moment?"

They were in a crowded square. The woman went toward an alleyway to the right of a shop and began to climb a staircase that smelled of slops.

"If only you could tell them to leave my son alone."

"Who?"

"The other cops. The ones around here. They never stop making trouble for him."

"What does he do?"

"He works."

"Doing what?"

"How should I know? . . . Can't be helped if the housework isn't done for you. I can't clean up after others all day long and do my own as well."

She went to open the window, since there was a strong stuffy smell, but the place wasn't that untidy. Except for a bed in one corner, the living-cum-dining room was almost attractive.

"What's all the to-do?" she asked, taking off her hat.

"Maria Serre can't be found."

73

" 'Course not. She's in Holland."

"They can't find her in Holland, either."

"Why do you want to find her?"

"We have reason to believe she's been murdered."

A tiny spark kindled in Eugénie's brown eyes.

"Why don't you arrest them?"

"We haven't any proof yet."

"And you're counting on me to get you some?"

She put some water to heat on the gas ring and came over to Maigret again.

"What happened on Tuesday?"

"She spent all day packing."

"Wait. She'd been married two and a half years, hadn't she? I suppose she had a good many things of her own."

"She had at least thirty dresses, and as many pairs of shoes."

"Was she smart?"

"She never threw anything out. Some of the dresses dated back ten years. She didn't wear them, but she wouldn't have given them away for all the money in the world."

"Stingy?"

"Aren't all rich people stingy?"

"I was told that all she took with her was a trunk and two suitcases."

"That's right. The rest went a week before."

"You mean she sent other trunks away?"

"Trunks, crates, cardboard boxes. A moving van came to get them all last Thursday or Friday."

"Did you look at the labels?"

"I don't remember the exact address, but it was to go to Amsterdam."

74

"Did your employer know?"

"Of course he did."

"So her departure had been decided on for some time?"

"Since her last attack. After each attack she'd talk about going back to her own country."

"What kind of attacks?"

"Heart, so she said."

"She had a weak heart?"

"Seems like it."

"Did a doctor come to see her?"

"Dr. Dubuc."

"Did she take any medicine?"

"After each meal. They all did. The other two still do. They each have a little bottle of pills or drops beside their plate."

"What's wrong with Guillaume Serre?"

"I don't know."

"And his mother?"

"Rich people always have something wrong with them."

"Did they get on well?"

"Sometimes they didn't speak to each other for weeks."

"Maria Serre wrote a lot of letters?"

"From morning till night."

"Did you ever happen to take them to the post office?"

"Often. They were always to the same person, a woman with a funny name, who lives in Amsterdam."

"Are the Serres well off?"

"I think so."

"What about Maria?"

"Of course. Otherwise he wouldn't have married her."

"Did you work for them when they got married?"

75

"No."

"You don't know who did the housework at that time?"

"They're always changing their daily help. . . . It's *my* last week now. Soon as a person sees what's what, she leaves."

"Why?"

"How would you like to have the lumps of sugar in the sugar bowl counted, and have a half-rotten apple picked out for your dessert?"

"Old Madame Serre?"

"Yes. Just because at her age she works all day—which is her own funeral—she's on you like a shot if you're unlucky enough to be caught sitting down for a moment."

"Does she scold you?"

"She's never scolded me. I'd like to see her! . . . It's far worse. She's only too polite. She looks at you in a down-hearted sort of way, as if it made her sad to see you."

"Did anything strike you when you got to work on Wednesday morning?"

"No."

"You didn't notice if a window had been broken during the night? Whether there was fresh putty around one of the panes?"

She nodded. "You've got the wrong day."

"Which day was it?"

"Four or five days before, when we had that big thunderstorm."

"You're sure of that?"

"Certain. I had to polish the floor of the study, because the rain came in."

"Who put in the pane?"

"Monsieur Guillaume."

"He went to buy it himself?"

"Yes. It was about ten o'clock in the morning. He had to go to the hardware store on rue de Longchamp. . . . They never have a workman in if they can do without one. Monsieur Guillaume unstops all the drains himself."

"You're sure about the date?"

"Absolutely."

"Thank you very much."

Maigret had no further business with her. There was really nothing more for him to do on rue de la Ferme, either. Unless, of course, Eugénie was merely repeating a piece she'd been taught to say. In that case, she was a better liar than most.

"You don't think they killed her, do you?" she asked.

He didn't answer, but went toward the door.

"Because of the windowpane?" There was a slight hesitation in her tone. "Does the window have to be broken on the day you said?"

"Why do you ask? Do you want to see them go to jail?"

"Nothing I'd like better. But, now that I've told the truth . . ."

She regretted saying that; for two pins she'd have gone back on it.

"You could always ask at the hardware store where he bought the glass and the putty."

"Thank you for the tip."

He stood for a moment in front of the shop outside, which happened to be a hardware store. But it wasn't the right one. He waited for a taxi.

"Rue de la Ferme."

There was no point in leaving Torrence and the Neuilly Inspector on the sidewalk there any longer. The recollection of Ernestine playing her little joke on rue de la Lune came back to him, and he didn't find it at all funny. She was the one responsible for this business. He'd been a fool to rush into it. Only this morning, in the Neuilly Superintendent's office, he'd made an ass of himself.

His pipe tasted foul. He crossed and uncrossed his legs. The partition was open between himself and the driver.

"Go around by rue de Longchamp. If the hardware store is still open, stop."

It was a toss-up. This would be his last throw. If the store was closed, he wouldn't bother to come back, in spite of Ernestine and Sad Freddie. Anyway, what proof was there that Alfred had really broken into the house on rue de la Ferme?

He'd gone off on his bicycle from Quai de Jemmapes, agreed, and at daybreak he'd telephoned his wife. But nobody really knew what they'd said to each other.

"It's open!"

Of course, the hardware store. A tall youth in a gray cotton jacket approached between galvanized tin pails and brooms to greet Maigret.

"Do you sell sheet glass?"

"Yes, sir."

"And putty?"

"Certainly. Have you brought the measurements?"

"It's not for myself. Do you know Monsieur Serre?"

"The dentist? Yes, sir."

"Is he a customer of yours?"

"He has an account here."

"Have you seen him recently?"

"*I* haven't, because I just got back from my vacation, day before yesterday. I can easily tell if he came in while I was away by looking in the book."

He didn't ask why, but went into the semidarkness of the back of the shop and opened a ledger that lay on a tall, raised desk.

"He bought a sheet of window glass last week."

"Which day?"

"Friday."

The thunderstorm had occurred on Thursday night. Eugénie had been right, as had old Madame Serre.

"He bought half a pound of putty, too."

"Thank you."

It hung by a thread, by an unthinking action on the part of the young man in the gray jacket, who would soon be shutting up the shop. He was turning over the pages of the ledger, more or less for form's sake.

"He came back again this week."

"What!"

"Wednesday. He bought a pane the same size, and another half pound of putty."

"You're sure?"

"I can even tell you that he came in early, because it's the first sale made that day."

"What time do you open?"

An important point, since, according to Eugénie, who started work at nine, all the windowpanes had been in good repair on Wednesday morning.

79

"Well, we get in at nine, but the boss comes down at eight to open the shop."

"Thanks. You're a bright boy."

The bright boy must have wondered for some time afterward why this man, who had looked so depressed when he came in, now seemed to be in high spirits.

"I suppose there's no danger of anyone destroying the pages in this ledger?"

"Why would anybody do that?"

"Why, indeed! All the same, I advise you to watch it. I'll send someone around tomorrow morning to photograph the pages."

He took a card from his pocket and handed it to the young man, who read with astonishment:

CHIEF INSPECTOR J. MAIGRET
POLICE JUDICIAIRE
PARIS

"Where to now?" asked the driver.

"Pull up for a moment on rue de la Ferme. You'll see a little bistro on your left. . . ."

This deserved a glass of beer. He nearly called Torrence and the other man to have one with him, but finally asked the driver to join him.

"What'll you have?"

"A white wine and Vichy."

The street was gilded by the sun. They could hear the breeze rustling through the big trees in the Bois de Boulogne.

There was a black wrought-iron gate farther up the road,

a green garden, a house as serene and well-ordered as a convent.

In that house lived an old woman like a mother superior and a sort of sultan with whom Maigret had a score to settle.

It was good to be alive.

5

The rest of the day went as follows. First of all, Maigret
drank two glasses of beer with the taxi driver, who had only
one white wine and Vichy water. By that time it was getting
cooler and, as he got back into the taxi, he had the notion
of driving around to the boardinghouse where Maria Van
Aerts had stayed for a year.

There was nothing in particular for him to do there. He
was simply following his habit of nosing around people's
homes in order to understand them better.

The walls were cream-colored. Everything was creamy,
luscious, as in a dairy, and the proprietress, with her floury
face, looked like a cake with too much icing on it.

"What a lovely person, Monsieur Maigret! And what a

wonderful companion she must have made for her husband!
. . . She wanted to get married so much."

"You mean she was looking for a husband?"

"Don't all young girls dream of a bridegroom?"

"She was about forty-eight when she lived here, if I'm
not mistaken."

"But she was still so young at heart! Anything could
make her laugh. . . . Would you believe it, she loved to
play practical jokes on her fellow guests. Near the Made-
leine, there's a shop I'd never noticed, before I found out
about it from her, that sells all sorts of novelty jokes: mechanical mice, spoons that melt in the coffee, gadgets that
you slide under the tablecloth to lift someone's plate up all
of a sudden, glasses that you can't drink from—I don't know
what all! Well, she was one of its best customers!

"A very cultured woman, all the same. She'd been to
every museum in Europe and used to spend whole days at
the Louvre."

"Did she introduce you to her prospective husband?"

"No. She was secretive by nature. . . . Perhaps she didn't
like to bring him here for fear that some of the others might
be envious. He was a man of very imposing presence. He
looked like a diplomat, I believe."

"Aha!"

"He's a dentist, she told me, but sees only a few patients,
by appointment. He belongs to a very rich family."

"And Mademoiselle Van Aerts herself?"

"Her father left her a good deal of money."

"Tell me, was she stingy?"

"Oh, you've heard about that? . . . She was certainly
thrifty. For instance, when she had to go into town, she'd

83

wait until one of the other guests was going too, so they could share a taxi. And every week she'd argue over her bill."

"Do you know how she came to meet Monsieur Serre?"

"I don't think it was through the matrimonial advertisement."

"She put an advertisement in the papers?"

"Not in earnest. She didn't believe in it. More for fun, really . . . I don't remember the exact wording, but something like 'Distinguished lady, foreign, wealthy, wishes to meet gentleman of similar circumstances, with a view to marriage.' She had hundreds of replies. She used to make dates with some, at the Louvre, sometimes in one gallery, sometimes in another. They had to carry a certain book, or wear a boutonniere."

There were other women like the proprietress, from England, Sweden, America, sitting in the wicker chairs in the lounge, from which the smooth hum of electric fans could be heard.

"I hope she hasn't come to any harm."

It was about seven o'clock when Maigret got out of the taxi at the Quai des Orfèvres. On the shady side of the street he'd caught sight of Janvier coming along, with a preoccupied expression, a package under his arm, and he'd waited to climb the stairs with him.

"How are things going, Janvier, my boy?"

"All right, Chief."

"What have you got there?"

"My dinner."

Janvier didn't grumble, but he had a martyred look.

"Why don't you go home?"

"Because of that woman Gertrude, damn her."

The offices, almost empty, were swept by drafts, because a breeze had come up and all the windows in the building were still open.

"I managed to track down Gertrude Oosting in Amsterdam. Or, rather, I got her maid on the phone. And then I had to dig up a fellow waiting for an identity card in the Aliens Section, to interpret, because the maid doesn't speak a word of French.

"As luck would have it, when I called back, the good Madame Oosting had gone out with her husband at four in the afternoon. There's some open-air concert there today, with a fancy-dress parade, and after that the Oostings are having dinner with friends; the maid doesn't know where. She has no idea when they'll be back, and she'd been told to put the children to bed.

"And, speaking of children . . ."

"What?"

"Nothing, Chief."

"Come on, out with it!"

"Doesn't matter . . . The wife's a bit disappointed. It's our oldest boy's birthday, and she's got a special dinner ready."

"Did you find out from the maid if Gertrude Oosting can speak French?"

"She can."

"Go on home."

"What?"

"Go home. Leave me those sandwiches. I'll stay here."

85

"Madame Maigret won't like that."

Janvier needed a little persuasion, but finally went rushing off to catch his train to the suburbs.

Maigret ate alone in his office, then went for a chat with Moers, in his laboratory. Moers left after nine, when it was completely dark.

"Sure you know what to do?"

"Yes, Chief."

Moers took a photographer with him, and masses of equipment. It wasn't strictly legal, but, with the knowledge that Guillaume Serre had bought two windowpanes, not one, that no longer mattered.

"Get me Amsterdam, please. . . ."

At the other end, the maid gabbled something, and he understood her to mean that Madame Oosting still hadn't come home.

Then he called his wife.

"Would you mind coming to have a drink at the Brasserie Dauphine? I've probably got another hour or so to wait here. Take a taxi."

It wasn't a bad evening. The two of them were as comfortable as outside a café on the Grands Boulevards, except that their view was blocked by the tall pale flight of steps leading to the Palais de Justice.

The forensic men ought to be at work now on rue de la Ferme. Maigret had given them instructions to wait until the Serres had gone to bed. Torrence was to mount guard in front of the house to prevent the others from being caught breaking into the garage, which couldn't be seen from the house, and giving the car a thorough examination. Moers and the photographer would take care of that:

fingerprints, samples of dust for analysis, the whole works.

"You look pleased with yourself."

"I can't complain."

He wasn't prepared to admit that a few hours earlier he had been far from such a good mood. Now he could enjoy his drinks, while Madame Maigret sipped her sparkling water.

He left her twice to go call Amsterdam from his office. Not until eleven-thirty did he hear a voice that was not the maid's and that answered him in French.

"I can't hear you very well."

"I said I'm calling from Paris."

"Oh! Paris!"

She had a strong accent, not unattractive.

"Police Judiciaire."

"Police?"

"Yes. I'm telephoning with reference to your friend Maria—Maria Serre, whose maiden name was Van Aerts. You know her, don't you?"

"Where is she?"

"I don't know. That's what I want to ask you. She often wrote to you?"

"Yes, often. I was supposed to meet her at the station Wednesday morning."

"Were you there?"

"Yes."

"Did she come?"

"No."

"She didn't wire or telephone you that she couldn't come when she'd planned?"

"No. And I'm worried."

87

"Your friend has disappeared."

"What do you mean?"

"What did she tell you in her letters?"

"Lots of things."

She began to speak in her own language to someone, probably her husband, who was evidently standing beside her.

"Do you think Maria is dead?"

"Maybe. Did she ever write to you that she was unhappy?"

"She was distressed."

"Why?"

"She didn't like the old lady."

"Her mother-in-law?"

"Yes."

"What about her husband?"

"It appears that he wasn't a man, just an overgrown schoolboy who was terrified of his mother."

"How long ago did she write that?"

"Almost as soon as she got married. A few weeks after."

"She talked about leaving him?"

"Not then. After about a year or so."

"And recently?"

"She'd made up her mind. She asked me to find her an apartment in Amsterdam, near ours."

"Did you find one for her?"

"Yes. And a maid."

"So it was all arranged?"

"Yes. I was at the station, as I said."

"Have you any objection to sending me copies of your friend's letters? Did you keep them?"

"I have kept all the letters, but it would be hard to copy them: they are very long. I can send you the ones that matter. You're sure something's happened to her?"

"I'm convinced of it."

"Murdered?"

"Possibly."

"Her husband?"

"I don't know. Listen, Madame Oosting, you could do me a great favor. Has your husband got a car?"

"Of course."

"It would be kind of you to drive to Central Police Headquarters, which is open all night. Tell the duty officer that you were expecting your friend Maria. Show him her last letter. Then tell him you're very worried and that you'd like the matter looked into."

"Should I mention your name?"

"It doesn't matter. What you must do is insist on an investigation."

"I will."

"Thank you. Don't forget the letters you promised to send me."

He called Amsterdam again almost at once, asking this time for Central Police Headquarters.

"In a few minutes, a Madame Oosting will be coming to see you about the disappearance of her friend Madame Serre, née Van Aerts."

"Did she disappear here?"

"No. In Paris. In order to take action, I need an official complaint. As soon as you've taken down her statement, I'd like you to send me a wire asking us to make inquiries."

This took a little time. The duty officer couldn't understand how Maigret, in Paris, knew that Madame Oosting was coming.

"I'll tell you that later. But I must have your wire. Send it priority. I need it in less than half an hour."

He went back to join Madame Maigret, who must have been uncomfortable sitting alone outside the brasserie.

"Are you through?"

"Not yet. I'll have one drink, and then we'll leave."

"Home?"

"To the office."

That always impressed her. She'd only rarely been within the walls of the Police Judiciaire and felt she didn't know how to behave there.

"You look as if you were having fun. One would think you were playing a joke on somebody."

"I am, in a way."

"On whom?"

"A fellow who looks like a sultan, a diplomat, and a schoolboy."

"I don't understand."

"Naturally not!"

He wasn't often in such high spirits. How many calvados had he drunk? Four? Five? Before going back to the office, he swallowed one more. Then he took his wife's arm to cross the couple of hundred yards along the quay.

"Just one thing: don't start telling me again that everything's covered with dust and that the offices need a good cleaning!"

On the telephone again: "Any telegrams come for me?"

"Nothing, Chief Inspector."

Ten minutes later, the whole squad, with the exception of Torrence, was back from rue de la Ferme.

"Did it go all right? No hitches?"

"No hitches. Nobody disturbed us. Torrence insisted we wait until the lights had all gone out in the house, and Guillaume Serre hung around for a long time before going to bed."

"The car?"

Vacher, who had nothing more to do, asked if he could go home. Moers and the photographer stayed behind. Madame Maigret, sitting on a chair as if paying a visit, assumed the abstracted expression of one who is not listening.

"We went over every bit of the car, which doesn't seem to have been taken out for two or three days. The gas tank's about half full. There are no signs of a struggle inside. In the trunk I found two or three more or less recent scratches."

"As if a large, heavy piece of luggage had been stowed in it?"

"That could be."

"A trunk, for instance?"

"A trunk or a crate."

"Were there any bloodstains inside?"

"No. No loose hairs, either. I thought of that. . . . We took a flashlight along, and there's a light plug in the garage. Emile is going to make enlargements."

"I'll do it right now," the photographer said. "If you could wait twenty minutes . . ."

"I'll wait. Did it look to you, Moers, as if the car had been cleaned lately?"

"Not on the outside. It hadn't been washed down by a

garage. But it looked as if the inside had been carefully brushed. Even the mat must have been beaten, because I had trouble finding any dust in it. Still, I've got several specimens for testing."

"Was there a brush in the garage?"

"No. I looked. They must have taken it away."

"So, except for the scratches—"

"Nothing out of the way . . . Can I go now?"

They were left alone, Madame Maigret and he, in the office.

"Aren't you sleepy?"

She said no. She had her own special way of looking at the surroundings in which her husband spent most of his life, of which she knew so little.

"Is it always like this?"

"What?"

"A case. When you don't come home."

She must have thought it was easy, quiet work, more like a kind of game.

"Depends."

"Has there been a murder?"

"More than likely."

"Do you know who did it?"

She turned her head away as he smiled at her. Then she asked: "Does he know that you suspect him?"

He nodded.

"Do you suppose he's asleep?"

After a moment, she added with a slight shiver: "It must be awful."

"I don't suppose it was fun for the poor woman, either."

"I know. But that was quicker, don't you think?"

"Maybe."

The telegram from the Dutch police came through on the phone, with a confirming copy promised for the next morning.

"Now, then! We can go home."

"I thought you were waiting for the photographs."

He smiled once more. Really, she'd have liked to find out. She didn't feel now like going back to bed.

"They won't tell us anything."

"Don't you think so?"

"I'm sure of it. Moers's laboratory tests won't either."

"Why not? Because the murderer was too careful?"

He did not reply, but put out the light and led his wife into the corridor, where the cleaners were at work.

"That you, Monsieur Maigret?"

He looked at the alarm clock, which said eight-thirty. His wife had let him sleep. He recognized Ernestine's voice.

"Did I wake you up?"

He preferred not to admit it.

"I'm at the post office. There's another card for me."

"From Le Havre?"

"From Rouen. He doesn't say anything, and still hasn't answered my advertisement. Nothing except my name and Poste Restante, same as yesterday."

There was a pause. Then she asked: "Have you heard anything?"

"Yes."

"What?"

"Something to do with windowpanes."

"Good?"

"Depends for whom."

"For us?"

"It may do Alfred and you some good."

"You don't still think I've been telling lies?"

"Not at the moment."

At the PJ, he picked Janvier to go with him and drive the little black police car.

"Rue de la Ferme."

With the telegram in his pocket, he had the car stop outside the wrought-iron gate, through which the two of them passed looking their most official. Maigret rang. A window curtain moved on the second floor, where the shutters were not yet closed.

It was Eugénie, in down-at-the-heel slippers, who came to the door, wiping her wet hands on her apron.

"Good morning, Eugénie. Monsieur Serre is at home, and I'd like a word with him."

Somebody leaned over the banister. The old woman's voice said: "Show the gentlemen into the drawing room, Eugénie."

It was the first time Janvier had been in the house, and he was impressed.

They heard footsteps overhead. Then the door opened abruptly, and the huge bulk of Guillaume Serre almost filled the entrance.

He was as self-possessed as ever, and stared at them with the same calm insolence.

"Have you a warrant?" he asked, his lip twitching slightly.

Maigret deliberately took some time getting his wallet

94

out of his pocket, opening it, and finding a document, which he handed over politely.

"Here you are, Monsieur Serre."

The man wasn't prepared for this. He read the form, then took it over to the window to decipher the signature, while Maigret was explaining.

"As you see, it's a search warrant. Inquiries have been instituted into the disappearance of Madame Maria Serre, née Van Aerts, on a complaint lodged by Madame Gertrude Oosting, of Amsterdam."

The old lady entered on these last words.

"What is it, Guillaume?"

"Nothing, Mama," he told her in a curiously gentle voice. "These gentlemen would, I believe, like to search the house. Go up to your room."

She wavered, looking at Maigret as if to ask his advice.

"You'll keep your temper, Guillaume?"

"Of course, Mama. Please leave us, I beg of you."

Things weren't going exactly as Maigret had foreseen. He frowned.

"I suppose," he said when the old lady had reluctantly left, "you'll want to consult your lawyer. I'll probably have a few questions to ask you later on."

"I don't need a lawyer. Now that you have a warrant, I cannot object to your presence here. That's that."

The shutters on the ground floor were closed, and they'd been in semidarkness. Serre walked toward the nearest window.

"No doubt you'd prefer more light on the scene."

He spoke in a flat voice and, if any expression at all could be read in his tone, it was one of contempt.

95

"Do your duty, gentlemen."

It came almost as a shock to see the drawing room in full daylight. Serre went into his study next door, where he also opened the shutters, then into his office.

"When you wish to go up to the second floor, please let me know."

Janvier was glancing in bewilderment at his chief. The latter wasn't quite so bouyant as he'd been that morning or the night before. He seemed to be worried.

"May I use your telephone, Monsieur Serre?" he asked with the same cold courtesy the other had shown him.

"You have every right to."

He dialed the PJ. Moers had made a verbal report that morning, which, as the Chief Inspector had expected, was more or less negative. The particles of dust had been analyzed with no result, or almost none. Moers had managed to scrape up, from the front of the car, by the driver's seat, only a minute quantity of powdered brick.

"Give me the laboratory. . . . That you, Moers? Can you come over to rue de la Ferme with your men and equipment?"

He was watching Serre, who, engaged in lighting a long black cigar, didn't bat an eyelid.

"Everything . . . No, there's no body. I'll be here."

Then, turning to Janvier: "You can get started."

"On this room?"

"Any one you like."

Guillaume Serre followed them step by step and watched what they were doing without a murmur. He had slipped on

96

a black alpaca jacket over his white shirt, but wore no tie.

While Janvier searched the desk drawers, Maigret went through the dentist's private files and made entries in his large notebook.

Really, it had begun to border on farce. He'd have been hard put to say precisely what he was looking for. What it amounted to in the end was seeing whether, at any given moment, in any particular part of the house, Serre would show a sign of uneasiness.

When they searched the drawing room, he had not moved a muscle, standing rigid and full of dignity, with his back to the brown marble mantelpiece.

Now he was watching Maigret as if wondering what the man could be searching for, but it seemed to be more out of curiosity than fear.

"You certainly have very few patients, Monsieur Serre."

He made no reply, just shrugged.

"I notice that there are far more women patients than men."

The other's expression seemed to say, "So what?"

"I also see that you first met Maria Van Aerts in your professional capacity."

He found entries for five visits, spaced over two months, with details of the treatment given.

"Were you aware that she was wealthy?"

A further shrug.

"Do you know Dr. Dubuc?"

He nodded.

"He was your wife's doctor, unless I'm mistaken. Did you recommend him to her?"

Wonders never cease! He talked at last!

"Dr. Dubuc was treating Maria Van Aerts before she became my wife."

"You knew, when you married her, that she had heart trouble?"

"She told me about it."

"Was it serious?"

"Dubuc will tell you, if he considers it his duty."

"Your first wife had a weak heart, too, hadn't she?"

"You'll find her death certificate in the files."

Janvier was more ill at ease than anyone. He greeted with relief the arrival of the technical experts, who would bring a little life into the house.

When their car drew up in front of the gate, Maigret went to open the door himself, and said to Moers under his breath: "The whole show. Go over the house with a fine-tooth comb."

Moers, who had understood and had spotted the bulky form of Guillaume Serre, muttered: "You think that'll shake him?"

"It might end up by shaking someone."

A few moments later one might have thought that auctioneers had taken over the house and were preparing to put it up for public sale. The men from the Forensic Lab left no corner untouched, taking down the pictures and the photographs, pushing back the piano and the armchairs to look underneath the carpets, piling up cupboard drawers, spreading out documents.

Once, they caught sight of the face of Madame Serre, who, after one glance through the doorway, withdrew with a look of distress. Then Eugénie came in, grumbling.

"You'll put everything back where it was, I hope."

She carried on much more when her kitchen was put through it, even the broom closets.

"If only you'd tell me what it is you're looking for."

They weren't looking for anything in particular. Perhaps, when it came to the point, even Maigret wasn't looking for anything at all. He was watching the man who followed in their tracks and never lost his poise for a second.

Why had Maria written to her friend that Serre was really nothing more than an overgrown schoolboy?

While his men continued to work, Maigret got Dr. Dubuc on the telephone.

"You won't be going out for a while? . . . Can I come and see you? . . . No, it won't take long. Thanks."

Dubuc had five patients in his waiting room, but had promised the Chief Inspector to let him in by the back door. It was a stone's throw away, along the quay. Maigret went there on foot. As he passed the hardware store, the young man he'd seen the day before hailed him.

"Aren't you going to photograph the ledger?"

"Soon."

Dubuc was about fifty, had a ginger beard, and wore glasses.

"You attended Madame Serre, didn't you, doctor?"

"Young Madame Serre. Or, rather, the younger of the two."

"You never attended anyone else in the house?"

"Let me see . . . Yes! A cleaning woman who'd cut her hand, two or three years ago."

"Was Maria Serre really ill?"

"She needed treatment, yes."

99

"Heart?"

"An enlarged heart. Moreover, she ate too much, and complained of dizziness."

"Did she often call you in?"

"About once a month. Other times, she came to see me."

"Did you prescribe any medicine for her?"

"A sedative, in pill form. Nothing toxic."

"You don't think she could have had a heart attack?"

"Most unlikely. In ten or fifteen years, perhaps . . ."

"Did she do anything to get her weight down?"

"Every four or five months she'd decide to go on a diet, but her resolution never lasted more than a few days."

"You've met her husband?"

"Occasionally."

"What do you think of him?"

"In what way? Professionally? One of my women patients went to him for treatment and told me that he was very skillful and very gentle."

"As a man?"

"I thought he seemed of a retiring disposition. What is all this about?"

"His wife has disappeared."

"Ah!"

Dubuc didn't give a damn, to tell the truth. He merely sketched a vague gesture.

"These things happen, don't they? He was wrong to ask the police to find her, because she'll never forgive him."

Maigret didn't argue the point. On his way back, he made a detour in order to pass the garage, which was no longer being watched. The house opposite had been divided into apartments. The concierge was outside on the step, polishing the brass knob on the front door.

"Does your window look out on the street?" he asked her.

"What's that got to do with you?"

"Police. Do you know the person who keeps his car in the garage opposite, the first one on the right."

"That's the dentist."

"You see him now and then?"

"I see him when he comes to get his car."

"Have you seen him this week?"

"Wait! . . . That reminds me. What was all that messing around in his garage last night? Was it burglars? I said to my husband—"

"It wasn't burglars."

"Was it you?"

"Never mind. Have you seen him take his car out this week?"

"I believe I did."

"Do you remember which day? What time?"

"It was one night, pretty late. Wait a minute. I'd got out of bed . . . Don't look at me like that. It'll come back to me."

She seemed to be doing some mental arithmetic.

"I'd just got out of bed, because my husband had a toothache, and went to get him an aspirin. If he was here, he'd tell you what day it was. I noticed Monsieur Serre's car coming out of the garage, and I remember saying what a coincidence."

"Because your husband had a toothache?"

"Yes. And there was a dentist across from the house at

101

that very moment. . . . It was after midnight. Mademoiselle Germains had come in. So it was Tuesday, because she only goes out on Tuesday nights, to play cards at some friends'."

"The car was coming out? It wasn't going in?"

"It was coming out."

"Which way did it go?"

"Toward the Seine."

"You didn't hear it stop a little farther on, at Monsieur Serre's house?"

"I didn't take any more notice of it. I was barefoot, and the floor was cold, because we sleep with the window half open. . . . What's he done?"

What could Maigret answer? He merely thanked her and left. After crossing the little garden, he rang. Eugénie opened the door, giving him a black, reproachful look.

"The gentlemen are upstairs," she told him curtly.

They'd finished with the ground floor. From upstairs noisy footsteps and the rumble of furniture being dragged across the floorboards could be heard.

Maigret went up, and found old Madame Serre sitting on a chair in the middle of the landing.

"I no longer know where to go," she said. "It's like moving. What can they be looking for, Monsieur Maigret?"

Guillaume Serre, standing in the center of a room flooded with sunlight, was lighting a fresh cigar.

"My goodness, why did we let her go!" sighed the old lady. "If I'd only known . . ."

She did not state precisely what she would have done had she foreseen the trouble that her daughter-in-law's disappearance would bring down upon her.

6

It was twenty to four when Maigret made up his mind, twenty-five past four when the questioning began. But the fateful, even dramatic moment was the moment when the decision was made.

Maigret's behavior had come as a surprise to those working with him in the house on rue de la Ferme. Ever since morning there had been something unusual about the way in which the Chief Inspector was directing operations. It wasn't the first search of this kind in which they'd taken part, but the more this one proceeded, the more it took on a different nature from any other. It was difficult to define. Janvier, because he knew his chief better than the others, was the first to feel the change.

When he had set them to work, there had been a slight, almost fierce, flicker of glee in Maigret's eyes; he had loosed them on the house as he might have loosed a pack of hounds on a fresh scent, urging them on, not by his voice, but by his whole attitude.

Had it become a personal matter between himself and Guillaume Serre? More precisely, would events have taken the same course, would Maigret have made the same decision, at the same moment, had the man on rue de la Ferme not been heavier than he physically, and so immovable?

Maigret had seemed, from the start, impatient to come to grips with him.

Later, different motives might have been attributed to him. Was he taking a more or less malicious pleasure in turning the house upside down?

They had seldom been given the chance to work in a home like this, where everything was peaceful, serene, harmonious in a muted minor key, where even the most outdated objects were in no way ludicrous—and where, after hours of exhaustive searching, they hadn't come across even one questionable detail.

When he made his decision at twenty to four, they still hadn't found anything. The search party was feeling somewhat uncomfortable, and was expecting the Chief to withdraw with apologies.

What was it that decided Maigret? Did he know himself? Janvier went so far as to suspect him of having drunk too many aperitifs when, about one o'clock, he'd gone to have a bite on the terrace of the bistro opposite. On his return, the smell of Pernod could be detected on his breath.

Eugénie hadn't set the table for her employers. Several times she'd gone up to whisper, now in the ear of Madame Serre, now in that of the dentist. They'd later caught sight of the mother eating while standing in the kitchen, as one might eat during the process of moving one's home. And, not long after that, the cleaning woman took up a sandwich and a cup of coffee for Guillaume.

They were working in the attic by then. This was the most personal part of the house, more personal than the bedrooms and the linen closets.

It was enormous. Dormer windows shed two large, luminous rectangles on the dingy floorboards. Janvier had opened two leather gun cases, and a ballistics man had examined the weapons.

"These belong to you?"

"They belonged to my father-in-law. I have never done any shooting."

An hour earlier, in Guillaume's room, they had found a revolver, which had been examined, and which Maigret had placed on the pile of objects to be taken away for further checking.

There was a little of everything in that pile, including the dentist's professional records and, from a writing desk in the old lady's room, the death certificates of her husband and her first daughter-in-law.

There was also a suit of clothing in whose sleeve Janvier had noticed a slight tear. Guillaume Serre claimed he'd not worn it for ten days.

They stumbled among old trunks, packing boxes, pieces of broken furniture. In a corner stood an old-fashioned high chair, with colored knobs on either side of the tray, and also a rocking horse, minus tail and mane.

They didn't stop working at lunchtime. The men took turns going for a bite; Moers was satisfied with a sandwich brought to him by the photographer.

Around two o'clock, Maigret got a call from the office, to tell him that a heavy envelope had just come by air from the Netherlands. He had it opened. Inside were Maria's letters, written in Dutch.

"Get hold of a translator and put him to work."

"Here?"

"Yes. He's not to leave the PJ until I come."

Guillaume Serre's demeanor had not changed. He'd followed them around, hadn't missed a single action or gesture, but not even once had he seemed agitated.

He had a special way of staring at Maigret; it was obvious that, for him, the others didn't count. It was indeed a match between the two, seemingly a personal combat. In the dentist's eyes could be seen an indefinable expression; it might be reproach or it might be contempt.

In any case, he didn't allow this large-scale operation to intimidate him. He raised no objections and submitted to this invasion of his home and privacy with lofty resignation; not the slightest trace of anxiety was perceptible.

Was he a weakling? A tough customer? Either description was plausible. His torso was that of a wrestler, his behavior that of a self-assured man, and yet, Maria's description of him as an overgrown schoolboy was not incongruous. His skin was pale, sickly. In a drawer they'd found a mass of doctor's prescriptions, pinned together in separate sheafs, some of them dating twenty years back. The family's med-

106

ical history could have been reconstructed with the help of these prescriptions, some of which were yellow with age. There was also, in the upstairs bathroom, a small white-painted cabinet containing bottles of patent medicine and boxes of pills both new and old.

In this house nothing was ever thrown away, not even old brooms, which were stacked in a corner of the attic beside cracked leather shoes that would never be of any use again.

Each time they left a room to launch an attack upon the next, Janvier gave his chief a look that meant: "Another washout!"

Janvier still expected to make some discovery, however. Did Maigret, on the other hand, rely on their finding nothing? He never seem surprised, watched them move ahead, puffing lazily at his pipe, and sometimes forgot for a whole quarter of an hour to glance at the dentist.

They realized his decision by implication, which made it strike them more forcibly.

Everybody was coming down from the attic, where Guillaume Serre was closing the dormer windows. His mother came out of her room to watch them go. But they all stood on the landing, in an uneasy group, surrounded by litter.

Maigret turned to Serre, when he joined them, and said, as if it were the most natural thing in the world: "Would you mind putting on a tie and a pair of shoes?"

Throughout the day, the man had been wearing his slippers.

Serre grasped his meaning, stared at him, undoubtedly surprised, but managed not to let it show. His mother opened her mouth to speak, either to protest or to demand an explanation, but Serre took her arm and led her back into her room.

Janvier asked under his breath: "You're arresting him?"

Maigret made no reply. He didn't know. To tell the truth, he'd only just made up his mind, on the spur of the moment, there on the landing.

"Come in, Monsieur Serre. Will you take a seat?"

The clock on the mantelpiece said four-twenty-five. It was Saturday. Maigret had realized this only from the bustle in the streets as they crossed the city in a police car.

The Chief Inspector closed the door. The windows were open, and papers on the desk fluttered under the weights that prevented them from blowing away.

"I asked you to sit down."

He went into the little wall closet to hang up his jacket and to rinse his hands under the faucet.

For the next ten minutes he didn't say a word to the dentist, but was busy signing things that were waiting on his desk. He rang for Joseph, and gave them to him. Then, slowly and deliberately, he filled the half-dozen pipes set out in front of him.

It was seldom that anyone in Serre's position could stand it for long without asking questions, losing his nerve, crossing and uncrossing his legs.

At last there was a knock at the door. It was the photographer who'd worked with them all day. He'd been sent on a mission by Maigret. He handed the Chief Inspector the still-damp print of a document.

"Thank you, Dambois. Don't leave without letting me know."

He waited until the door closed again, and lit one of the pipes.

"Would you bring your chair nearer, Monsieur Serre?"

They were now facing each other, separated by the width of the desk, across which Maigret held out the document in his hand.

He added no comment. The dentist took the print, got a pair of eyeglasses out of his pocket, examined it carefully, and put it down.

"I'm waiting."

"I have nothing to say."

The photograph was of a page from the hardware-store ledger, the one recording the sale of the second pane of glass and the second half-pound of putty.

"You realize what that implies?"

"Am I to understand that I'm being charged?"

Maigret hesitated.

"No," he decided. "Officially, you're summoned as a witness. If you wish, however, I am ready to charge you; more exactly, to ask the Public Prosecutor to indict you, which would entitle you to have legal advice."

"I've already told you that I don't want a lawyer."

These were only preliminary moves. Two heavyweights were sizing each other up, taking each other's measure, feeling their way. The office had become a sort of ring, and silence reigned in the duty room, where Janvier had explained the situation to his colleagues.

"I bet we're in for a long session," he told them.

"Think the Chief'll go the limit?"

"He's got that look on his face."

They all knew what that meant, and Janvier was the first

to call his wife and tell her not to be surprised if he didn't come home that night.

"Have you a weak heart, Monsieur Serre?"

"An enlarged heart—like you, in all probability."

"Your father died of heart trouble when you were seventeen, didn't he?"

"Seventeen and a half."

"Your first wife died of heart trouble. Your second wife also had heart trouble."

"According to statistics, about thirty percent of people die of heart failure."

"Your life's insured, Monsieur Serre?"

"Since I was a child."

"Of course. I saw the policy earlier. If I remember rightly, your mother is not insured."

"That's correct."

"Your father was?"

"I believe so."

"And your first wife?"

"I saw you take the documents."

"Your second wife, as well?"

"It's quite usual."

"What is less usual is to keep a sum of several million francs, in gold and currency, in a safe."

"Do you think so?"

"Can you tell me why you keep this money at home, where it brings in no interest?"

"I think thousands of people, nowadays, do the same. You forget the financial events that have resulted several times in panic, the excessive rate of taxation, and the constant devaluations. . . ."

"I understand. You admit that your intention was to conceal your capital and defraud the Treasury?"

Serre was silent.

"Did your wife—I mean your second wife, Maria—know this money was in your safe?"

"She did."

"You told her about it?"

"Her own money was there as well, a few days ago."

He took his time before answering these questions, weighed his words, let them fall one by one while keeping his eyes fixed gravely on the Chief Inspector.

"I didn't find any marriage contract among your papers. Am I to conclude that you were married under the joint-ownership laws?"

"That is correct."

"Isn't that odd, considering your ages?"

"I have already given you the reason. A contract would have obliged us to draw up a balance sheet of our respective property."

"Therefore, the joint ownership had no existence in actual fact?"

"We each continued to retain control of our own affairs."

And didn't all this seem quite natural?

"Was your wife wealthy?"

"She is wealthy."

"As wealthy as you are, or wealthier?"

"About the same."

"Does she have all of her money in France?"

"Only part of it. From her father, she inherited shares in a cheese factory in the Netherlands."

"In what form did she keep her other assets?"

111

"Mainly in gold."

"Even before she met you?"

"I see what you're getting at. Nevertheless, I will tell you the truth. It was I who advised her to sell her securities and to buy gold."

"This gold was kept, with yours, in your safe?"

"It used to be."

"Until when?"

"Tuesday. At the beginning of the afternoon, when she was nearly finished packing, she came downstairs, and I gave her what belonged to her."

"Then, when she left, it was in one of the two suitcases or in the trunk?"

"I suppose so."

"She didn't go out before dinner?"

"I didn't hear her go out."

"So, to your knowledge, she didn't go out?"

He nodded in confirmation.

"Did she telephone at all?"

"The only telephone in the house is in my study, and she did not use it."

"How am I to know, Monsieur Serre, that the money I found in the safe is yours alone, and not yours *and* your wife's?"

Without emotion, still maintaining an expression of weariness or disdain, the dentist took from his pocket a green notebook, which he handed to the Chief Inspector. Its pages were covered with tiny figures. Those on the left-hand side were headed with the initial O; those on the right with the initial M.

"What does O stand for?"

"Ours. I mean my mother and me. We've always shared everything, without making any distinction between what is hers and what is mine."

"The M, I suppose, stands for Maria?"

"That is correct."

"I see a certain figure that occurs at regular intervals."

"Her share of the household expenses."

"Every month she paid you for her bed and board?"

"If you like. Actually, she didn't pay me any money, because it was in the safe, but her account was debited with the amount."

Maigret leafed through the notebook for a few minutes without speaking. Then he got up and went into the room next door, where, like schoolboys, the inspectors immediately pretended to be busy.

He gave instructions to Janvier in a low voice. Hesitating about whether he should have beer sent up, he swallowed, without thinking, what was left in a glass on Vacher's desk.

When he returned, Serre, who had not moved from his chair, now lit one of his long cigars and murmured, not without insolence: "Do you mind?"

Maigret, unwilling to say yes, shrugged.

"You have thought about this second windowpane, Monsieur Serre?"

"I haven't bothered to."

"You're wrong. It would be much better if you could find some reasonable explanation."

"I'm not looking for one."

"Do you continue to maintain that you replaced the pane in your study window once only?"

"The day after the thunderstorm."

113

"Would you like us to have the Weather Bureau confirm that there was no thunderstorm in Neuilly on Tuesday night?"

"It would be pointless. Unless it would give you some satisfaction. I'm speaking of last week's thunderstorm."

"The day after, you went to the hardware store on rue de Longchamp and bought a pane of glass and some putty?"

"I told you that already."

"You are prepared to swear that you have not been back to the shop since then?"

He pushed across the desk the photograph of the ledger entry.

"Why, in your opinion, would they enter a purchase of glass and putty twice in their account book?"

"I have no idea."

"Why would the owner put in his account book that you came in on Wednesday, about eight o'clock in the morning?"

"That's his business."

"When did you last use your car?"

"Sunday."

"Where did you go?"

"We took a drive for two or three hours, my mother and I, as we do every Sunday."

"In which direction?"

"Toward the Forest of Fontainebleau."

"Did your wife go with you?"

"No. She wasn't feeling well."

"You'd decided to separate?"

"There was no question of a separation. She was tired, run-down. She didn't always get along with my mother. By

114

mutual agreement, we decided that she would return to her own country for a few weeks, or a few months."

"She took her money with her?"

"Yes."

"Why?"

"Because there was a possibility that she wouldn't come back. We are no longer children. We are able to look at life calmly. We are making an experiment."

"You know, of course, Monsieur Serre, that there are two borders to cross before you reach Amsterdam. And French Customs, on the way out, is fairly strict about the currency regulations. Wasn't your wife afraid that her gold would be discovered and impounded?"

"Am I obliged to answer?"

"I think it's in your own interest."

"Even if I risk being indicted as an accomplice?"

"That would be less serious than a charge of murder."

"Very well. One of my wife's suitcases had a false bottom."

"Made especially for this trip?"

"No."

"She'd already had occasion to use it?"

"Several times."

"To cross the border?"

"The Belgian border and, once, the Swiss. You're aware, I'm sure, that until just recently it was easier and less expensive to procure gold in Belgium and, especially, in Switzerland."

"You admit your complicity in these transfers of capital?"

"I do."

Maigret got up and went back into the duty room.

115

"Mind coming in a moment, Janvier?"

To Serre, he said: "My inspector will take down this part of our interview. Please repeat to him, word for word, what you just told me. Have him sign his statement, Janvier."

He went out again, and Vacher showed him to the office assigned to the translator, who was a little man with glasses. He was making his translation by using one of the office typewriters, pausing from time to time to consult the dictionary he'd brought with him.

There were at least forty letters, and most of them were several pages long.

"Where did you begin?"

"At the beginning. I'm on the third letter. All three are from about two and a half years ago. . . . In the first one, the lady tells her friend she's getting married, that her future husband is a distinguished man, of imposing appearance, belonging to the highest French professional class; that his mother looks like . . . I can't remember which painting in the Louvre. I can tell you the name of the painter."

He turned the pages.

"A Clouet . . . Painting is mentioned all the time in these letters. When she's saying what the weather's like, she cites Monet or Renoir."

"I'd like you to work backward from the end now."

"As you wish. You realize that, even if I spend all night at it, I won't be through by tomorrow morning?"

"That's why I'm asking you to begin at the end. What's the date of the last letter?"

"Last Sunday."

"Can you read it to me quickly?"

"I can give you some idea of it. . . ."

Gertrude darling,

Paris has never been so resplendent as this morning, and I very nearly went with G. and his mother to the Forest of Fontainebleau, which must be adorned with all the glories of a Corot or a Courbet—

"Is there a lot about the glories?"

"Shall I skip?"

"Please."

The translator ran his eyes down a page, moving his lips silently, as if in prayer.

"Here you are."

I wonder what effect returning once again to our Netherlands and its pastel shades will have upon me, and, now that the time comes near, I feel I'm being cowardly.

After all that I've written to you about my life here, about G. and my mother-in-law, you must be wondering what has happened to me and why I am no longer happy.

It's perhaps because of the dream I had last night, which has spoiled my day. Do you recall the little picture that hangs in The Hague museum and made us blush? It isn't signed. It's attributed to a painter of the Florentine school whose name I have forgotten, and depicts a faun carrying over his shoulder a completely naked woman, who is resisting. Do you remember?

The faun, in my dream, had G.'s face, and his expression was so fierce that I woke up trembling and bathed in perspiration.

Not with fear—that was the strangest thing. My memory is confused. There was some fear, certainly, but also another emotion. I'll try to explain it to you on Wednesday, when we'll at

117

last be able to chat as we did so much when you came on your last trip.

I'm to leave on Tuesday night. It's settled. There's no doubt about it. So there are only two more days to wait. I have so many things to do during that time, it will pass quickly. Nevertheless, it still seems to me far away, almost unreal.

Sometimes I have the feeling, especially after that dream, that something will happen to prevent my departure.

Don't worry. My decision is final. I shall follow your advice. I cannot stand this life here for much longer. But—

"You in here, Chief?"

It was Janvier, with sheets of paper in his hand.

"It's done. He's waiting for you."

Maigret took the sheets, left the translator to his work, and crossed the duty room deep in thought.

Nobody, at that time, could have guessed how long the questioning would take.

Guillaume Serre looked up as the Chief Inspector returned. Of his own accord he took a pen from the desk.

"I suppose I have to sign?"

"Yes. Here. Have you read it through?"

"I've read it. May I trouble you for a glass of water?"

"Would you prefer red wine?"

The dentist looked at him, gave the faintest of smiles, inscrutable, heavy with irony and bitterness.

"That, too?" he said disdainfully.

"That, too, Monsieur Serre. You're so afraid of your mother that you are reduced to hiding to have a drink."

"Is that a question I have to answer?"

"Answer if you wish."

118

"Allow me to inform you, then, that my mother's father was a drunkard, that her two brothers, who are now dead, were drunkards, and that her sister ended her days in a mental institution. My mother has lived in fear of seeing me take to drink, in my turn; she refuses to believe that this tendency is not hereditary. When I was a student, she waited for my return with anxiety, and sometimes she even watched the cafés on Boulevard St.-Michel where I was sitting with my friends. There has never been any liquor in our home, and, though there's wine in the cellar, she continues the habit of carrying the key on her."

"She allows you a glass of wine with water at every meal, doesn't she?"

"I know that she came to see you and spoke to you."

"Did she tell you what she said to me?"

"Yes."

"Are you very fond of your mother, Monsieur Serre?"

"The two of us have almost always lived together."

"Rather like a married couple?"

He colored slightly.

"I don't know what you mean."

"Is your mother jealous?"

"I beg your pardon?"

"I'm asking you whether, as often happens with a widow and an only son, your mother shows signs of jealousy toward the people you know. . . . Have you many friends?"

"Has this any connection with the alleged disappearance of my wife?"

"I didn't find, in your house, a single letter from a friend, or even one of those group photographs one usually sees."

There was no response.

119

"Nor is there any photograph of your first wife."

Still silence.

"Another thing that struck me, Monsieur Serre: the portrait hanging over the mantelpiece is surely that of your maternal grandfather."

"Yes."

"The one who drank?"

A sign of assent.

"In a drawer, I came across a number of pictures of you as a child and as a young man; also pictures of women and men who must have been your grandmother, your aunt, and your uncles. All on your mother's side, apparently. Doesn't it seem surprising to you that there isn't a single portrait of your father or of his family?"

"It hadn't struck me."

"Were they destroyed after your father's death?"

"My mother could answer that question better than I."

"You don't remember if they were destroyed?"

"I was quite young."

"You were seventeen. . . . What do you remember about your father, Monsieur Serre?"

"Is this part of your interrogation?"

"Neither my questions nor your answers—as you see—are being recorded. Your father was a lawyer?"

"Yes."

"Did he take personal charge of his practice?"

"Not often. His chief clerk did most of the work."

"Did he lead a very social life? Or was he exclusively devoted to the family circle?"

"He went around a great deal."

"He had mistresses?"

"I couldn't tell you."

"Did he die in his bed?"

"On the stairs, going up to his room."

"Were you at home?"

"I'd gone out. When I came back, he'd been dead for nearly two hours."

"Who attended him?"

"Dr. Dutilleux."

"Is he still alive?"

"He died at least ten years ago."

"Were you there when your first wife died?"

He drew his heavy brows together, stared at Maigret fixedly, and his lower lip thrust out in a kind of disgust.

"Answer me, please."

"I was in the house."

"What part of the house?"

"In my study."

"What time was it?"

"About nine o'clock at night."

"Was your wife in her room?"

"She'd gone up early. She didn't feel well."

"Had she felt ill for some time?"

"I don't remember."

"Was your mother with her?"

"She was upstairs, too."

"With her?"

"I have no idea."

"Was it your mother who called you?"

"I think so."

"When you got to the room, your wife was dead?"

"No."

121

"Did she die soon afterward?"

"Fifteen or twenty minutes later. The doctor was just ringing the doorbell."

"Which doctor?"

"Dutilleux."

"He was your family doctor?"

"He took care of me when I was a child."

"A friend of your father?"

"Of my mother."

"Did he have children?"

"Two or three."

"You've lost sight of them?"

"I never knew them personally."

"Why didn't you inform the police that somebody had tried to break open your safe?"

"I had nothing to tell the police."

"What did you do with the tools?"

"What tools?"

"The ones the burglar left in the room when he made his escape."

"I saw neither tools nor burglar."

"Did you make use of your car on Tuesday night or early Wednesday morning?"

"I did not."

"You were unaware that somebody used it?"

"I have had no reason, since then, to go into the garage."

"When you put your car in the garage last Sunday, were there scratches on the trunk and the right fender?"

"I didn't notice anything."

"Did you get out of the car, you and your mother, during your drive?"

No answer.

"I asked you a question."

"I'm trying to remember."

"It shouldn't be so difficult. You were driving along the road to Fontainebleau. Did you set foot on the ground?"

"Yes. We went for a walk in the country."

"You mean on a country road?"

"A little path running between fields on the right-hand side of the road."

"Could you find this path again?"

"I think so."

"Was it paved?"

"I don't believe it was. . . . No. That seems unlikely."

"Where is your wife, Monsieur Serre?"

And the Chief Inspector rose, not expecting any answer.

"Because we've got to find her, haven't we?"

7

About five o'clock Maigret, who had got up for a moment to open the communicating door between his office and the duty room, winked at Janvier. A little later, he got up again to shut the window, despite the heat, because of the noise outside.

At ten minutes to six he passed through the duty room, his jacket over his arm.

"All yours!" he told Janvier.

The Inspector and his colleagues had grasped the situation quite a while ago. From the moment when, on rue de la Ferme, the Chief Inspector had ordered Serre to come along, Janvier was pretty sure that he wouldn't get away from the PJ very easily. What surprised him was that the

Chief had made his decision so abruptly, without waiting to have all the evidence in his hands.

"She's in the waiting room," he said under his breath.

"Who?"

"The mother."

Maigret stationed Marlieux, a young inspector who knew shorthand, behind the door.

"Same questions?" asked Janvier.

"The same. And any others that come into your head."

The idea was to wear down the dentist. The inspectors could take turns, go out for a cup of coffee or a drink, make contact with the outside world again, while Serre would stay as long as need be in the same office, in the same chair.

Maigret stopped first to see the translator, who'd decided to take off his jacket and tie.

"What's she saying?"

"I've translated the last four letters. There's a passage in the next to last that might interest you."

I've made up my mind, Gertrude dear. I am still wondering how it came about. Yet I had no dreams last night, or, if I had, I have forgotten them.

."Does she say much about her dreams?"

"Yes. They're always coming into it. And she interprets them."

"Go on."

You've often asked me what has gone wrong, and I answered that you were imagining things and that I was happy. The truth is that I was trying to persuade myself of it.

Honestly, I've done all I could, for two and a half years, to believe that this house is my home and that G. is my husband.

In my heart, you see, I knew that it wasn't true, that I'd always be a stranger here, more of a stranger than I was in the boardinghouse, where we two spent so many happy hours.

How did I suddenly come to see things as they really are?

Do you remember how, when we were little girls, we used to play at comparing everything we saw—people, streets, animals— with the illustrations in our picture books? We wanted life to be like them. Later, when we began to visit museums, it was paintings that we used for comparison.

I did the same here, I did it on purpose, without really believing in it, but this morning I suddenly saw the house as it really is. I saw my mother-in-law, I saw G. with clear vision, without illusions.

I hadn't had any for some time—I mean illusions. You've got to understand me. I no longer had any, but I stubbornly refused to admit it.

Now that's over. I made up my mind to leave on the spot. I haven't told anyone yet. The old lady hasn't any inkling. She still behaves the same toward me, meek and smiling, as long as I do everything she wants.

She's the most selfish woman I have ever known.

"Those words are underlined," the translator remarked. "Shall I go on?"

As for G., I wonder whether it won't be a relief for him to see me go. He knew from the beginning we had nothing in common. I could never get used to the feel of his skin, to his

126

smell. Do you understand now why we've never shared the same room, which surprised you so much?

After two and a half years, it's exactly as though I'd just met him in the street or in the Métro, and I have the same feeling of revulsion whenever he comes to my room. Luckily, that doesn't happen often.

I even think, between ourselves, that he comes only because he believes it gives me pleasure, or because he feels it's his duty.

Perhaps it's his mother who tells him to. It's possible. Don't laugh. I don't know how it is with your husband, but G. has the crestfallen look of a schoolboy who's just been given a hundred lines to do. Can you see what I mean?

I've often wondered if he was the same with his first wife. Probably. He would be the same, I think, with anyone. These people, you see—I mean the mother and son—live in a world of their own and have no need of anybody else.

It seems astonishing that the old woman once had a husband. They never speak about him. Besides themselves, there's nobody in the world except the people whose pictures are on the walls, people who are dead, but whom they talk about as if they were more alive than anyone on earth.

I can't stand it any longer, Gertrude. I'll talk to G. soon. I'll tell him I feel the need to breathe the air of my own country. He'll understand. What I'm wondering is how he'll pluck up the courage to tell his mother.

"Is there much more?" asked Maigret.

"Seven pages."

"Go on translating. I'll be back."

At the door he turned.

"When you're hungry or thirsty, call down to the Brasserie Dauphine. Get them to send up anything you want."

"Thank you."

From the corridor he saw, in the glass-paneled waiting room, old Madame Serre sitting on one of the green velvet chairs. She was bolt upright, her hands folded in her lap. When she caught sight of Maigret, she started to get up, but he passed without stopping and went down the stairs.

The examination had barely begun, yet it already was surprising to see life going on outside, in bright sunlight, people walking to and fro, taxis, buses with men on the platform reading the evening paper on their way home.

"Rue Gay-Lussac!" he told a driver. "I'll tell you where to stop."

The tall trees in the Luxembourg gardens swayed in the breeze. All the chairs were taken; there were a lot of bright dresses; some children were playing along the paths.

"Is Maître Orin at home?" he asked the concierge.

"He hasn't been out for over a month, poor man."

Maigret had thought of him suddenly. He was probably the oldest lawyer in Paris. The Chief Inspector had no idea of his age, but he'd always known him as an old man and a semi-invalid, which didn't stop the man from always having a smiling face and talking about women with a wicked twinkle in his eye.

He lived, with a housekeeper almost as old as he was, in an apartment cluttered with books and prints, which he collected. Most of the prints dealt with bawdy subjects.

Orin was seated in an armchair in front of the open window, his knees covered by a lap robe despite the weather.

128

"Well, my boy! What a pleasant surprise! I'd begun to think everyone had forgotten me, or thought I'd been laid to rest in Père-Lachaise long ago. What's the trouble this time?"

He didn't try to deceive himself, and Maigret colored slightly, since it was true that he'd seldom called on the lawyer for anything other than selfish reasons.

"I wondered if, by any chance, you ever knew a man named Serre, who, if I'm not mistaken, died thirty-two or thirty-three years ago."

"Alain Serre?"

"He was a lawyer."

"That would be Alain."

"What sort of man was he?"

"I suppose I'm not allowed to ask what it's all about?"

"About his son."

"I never saw the boy. I knew there was a son, but I never met him. You see, Maigret, Alain and I belonged to a lively set, for whom family life wasn't the be-all and end-all. Life for us didn't revolve around the family hearth. We were to be found mostly at our club or backstage at variety shows. We knew all the chorus girls by their Christian names."

He added, with a ribald grin: "If you know what I mean!"

"Did you ever meet his wife?"

"I must have been introduced to her. Didn't she live somewhere in Neuilly? . . . For some years, Alain was out of circulation. He wasn't the only one that happened to. There were even a few who looked down on us, once they got married. . . . I didn't expect to see him again. But then, a long time afterward—"

"About how long?"

"Let me see. The club had already moved from Faubourg St.-Honoré to avenue Hoche. Ten years? Twelve years? Anyway, he came back to us. . . . He behaved oddly at first, as if he thought we bore him a grudge for dropping us."

"Then?"

"Nothing. He soon redoubled the pace. Let's see . . . He went around for a long time with a little singer who had a big mouth. We had a nickname for her . . . something dirty. . . . I can't call it to mind."

"Did he drink?"

"Not more than anyone else. Two or three bottles of champagne occasionally . . ."

"What became of him?"

"What becomes of us all in the end. He died."

"That's all?"

"If you want to know the sequel, my boy, you'll have to ask aloft. It's St. Peter's business, not mine. What misdeed has his son committed?"

"I don't know yet. His wife has disappeared."

"A playboy?"

"No. Quite the reverse."

"Juliette! Bring us something to drink."

Maigret had to stay another quarter of an hour with the old man, who insisted on trying to find, among his prints, a sketch of the singer.

"I wouldn't swear that it's a good likeness. But a very talented fellow did it, one night when all of us were up in his studio."

The girl was naked and walking on her hands. Her face could not be seen because her hair was sweeping the floor.

"Come and see me again, Maigret my boy. If you'd had time to share my humble meal . . ."

A bottle of wine was warming in a corner of the room, and a pleasant smell of cooking filled the apartment.

The police in Rouen had not been able to find Sad Freddie, any more than those at Le Havre. Perhaps the expert safecracker was no longer in that town. Was he on his way back to Paris? Had he read Ernestine's message?

Maigret had sent an inspector on a mission along the riverbank.

"Where shall I start?"

"As far upstream as you can."

He'd also telephoned his wife to say he wouldn't be back for dinner.

"Do you think I'll see you tonight?"

"Probably not."

He wasn't hoping for too much. He knew that he'd assumed a big responsibility by rushing things and bringing Guillaume Serre to the Police Judiciaire before he had the slightest proof.

Now it was too late. He could no longer let him go.

He felt drowsy, glum. He sat down on the terrace of the Brasserie Dauphine, but, after reading right through the menu, he ordered only a sandwich and a glass of beer; he wasn't hungry.

Then he went slowly up the staircase. The lights had just come on, although it was still daylight. As his head reached the third-floor level, he glanced automatically at the waiting room. The first thing that caught his eye was a green hat, one that had begun to get on his nerves.

131

Ernestine was there, sitting opposite Madame Serre, with her hands in her lap like the old lady, and the same air of patience and resignation. She saw him but deliberately assumed a fixed stare, giving only a slight shake of her head.

He understood that she was asking him not to recognize her. Immediately, she began talking to the old lady as though the ice had been broken some time before.

He shrugged and pushed open the door of the duty room. The stenographer was at work, a pad of paper on his knee. The weary voice of Janvier could be heard, punctuated by his footsteps as he paced up and down the room next door.

"According to you, Monsieur Serre, your wife went to get a taxi on the corner of Boulevard Richard-Wallace. How long was she away?"

Before taking over from the Inspector, Maigret climbed up to Moers's attic, where the latter was busy filing documents.

"Tell me again: apart from the brick dust, there were no traces of anything else in the car?"

"The car had been cleaned out very thoroughly."

"You're sure?"

"It's only by chance that I found a little powdered brick in a fold of the mat under the driver's seat."

"Suppose the car hadn't been cleaned, and the driver had got out on a country road."

"A paved road?"

"No. Suppose, I'm saying, he got out, and a person with him, that they'd gone for a walk on the path and then got back into the car."

"And it hadn't been cleaned afterward?"

"That's right."

132

"There'd be marks left. Maybe not many. But I'd have found them."

"That's all I wanted to know. Don't leave yet."

"By the way, I found two hairs in the room of the woman who's disappeared. She was a natural blond, but gave herself henna rinses. I can tell you what face powder she used, too."

The Chief Inspector went downstairs again and this time into his office, throwing off his jacket. He had smoked a pipe in there all afternoon. Janvier had smoked cigarettes, and Serre cigars. The air was blue with smoke drifting in a haze up near the light.

"Are you thirsty, Monsieur Serre?"

"The Inspector gave me a glass of water."

Janvier left.

"Wouldn't you prefer a glass of beer? Or wine?"

Still the air of bearing Maigret a personal grudge for these little traps.

"Thank you all the same."

"A sandwich?"

"Do you expect to keep me here much longer?"

"I don't know. Probably. It'll depend on you."

He went to the door and called out: "Could one of you get me a road map of the Fontainebleau area?"

He took his time. All this was merely scratching the surface.

"When you go to eat, get them to send up some sandwiches and beer, Janvier."

"Yes, Chief."

The road map was brought to him.

"Show me the spot where you stopped on Sunday."

Serre searched for a moment or two, took a pencil from the desk, and marked a cross where the main road met a country lane.

"If there's a farm with a red roof on the left, this is the lane, here."

"How long did you walk?"

"About a quarter of an hour."

"Were you wearing the same shoes as today?"

He pondered, looked at his shoes, then nodded.

"You're sure about that?"

"Certain."

His shoes had rubber heels, on which concentric circles were stamped around the maker's name.

"Don't you think, Monsieur Serre, that it would be simpler and less tiring for you to tell the truth? When did you kill your wife?"

"I didn't kill her."

Maigret sighed, went to give more instructions next door. Couldn't be helped! It would probably take hours more. The dentist's complexion was slightly paler than in the morning, and dark circles had begun to show under his eyes.

"Why did you marry her?"

"My mother advised me to."

"Why?"

"For fear I'd be left alone someday. She thinks that I'm still a child and that I need someone to look after me."

"To stop you from drinking?"

Silence.

"I don't suppose your marriage with Maria Van Aerts was a love match, was it?"

134

"We were both nearly fifty."

"When did you start to quarrel?"

"We never quarreled."

"What did you do with your evenings, Monsieur Serre?"

"I?"

"You."

"I read mostly, in my study."

"And your wife?"

"Writing, in her room. She used to go to bed early."

"Did your father lose much money?"

"I don't understand."

"Have you ever heard that your father used to lead what they called in those days a fast life?"

"He went around a great deal."

"Did he spend large amounts of money?"

"I believe so."

"Your mother made scenes?"

"We're not the kind of people to make scenes."

"How much did your first marriage bring you?"

"We don't speak the same language."

"You and your first wife were married under the joint-ownership law?"

"That is correct."

"And she had money. So you must have inherited it."

"Is that unusual?"

"So long as your second wife's body isn't found, you can't inherit from her."

"Why shouldn't she be found alive?"

"You believe that, Monsieur Serre?"

"I didn't kill her."

"Why did you take your car out on Tuesday night?"

135

"I didn't take it out."

"The concierge in the house opposite saw you. It was around midnight."

"You forget that there are three garages, three former stables, whose doors are adjacent. It was at night; you say so yourself. She may have got them confused."

"The man in the hardware shop couldn't have mistaken someone else for you, in broad daylight, when you went in to buy putty and another windowpane."

"My word's as good as his."

"Provided you didn't kill your wife . . . What did you do with the trunk and the suitcases?"

"That's the third time I've been asked that question. You've forgotten to mention the tools this time."

"Where were you on Tuesday about midnight?"

"In bed."

"Are you a light sleeper, Monsieur Serre?"

"No. My mother is."

"Neither of you heard anything?"

"I seem to remember telling you that already."

"And on Wednesday morning you found the house as usual?"

"I suppose that, since this is now an official inquiry, you have the right to question me. And you've decided to put me through an endurance test, haven't you? Your inspector has already asked me all these questions. Now you've started all over again. . . . I can see that it's going to go on all night. To save time, I'll tell you once and for all that I didn't kill my wife. I also inform you that I will not answer any questions that have already been put to me. . . . Is my mother here?"

"What makes you think she is?"

"Does it seem peculiar to you?"

"She's sitting in the waiting room."

"Do you mean to let her spend the night there?"

"I'll make no attempt to prevent her. She's quite free."

This time Guillaume Serre looked at him with hatred.

"I wouldn't like to have your job."

"I wouldn't like to be in your shoes."

They stared at each other in silence, each determined not to lower his gaze.

"You killed your wife, Serre. As you probably killed the first one."

The other didn't move a muscle.

"You'll confess to it."

A contemptuous smile curled the dentist's lips, and he threw himself back in his chair and crossed his legs.

Next door, the waiter from the Brasserie Dauphine could be heard putting plates and glasses on a desk.

"I wouldn't mind something to eat."

"Perhaps you'd like to take off your coat."

"No."

He started to eat a sandwich slowly, while Maigret went to fill a glass with water from the sink in the wall closet.

It was eight o'clock in the evening.

They could watch the windows darkening gradually, the view dissolving into specks of light that seemed as far away as the stars.

Maigret had to send out for tobacco. At eleven o'clock the dentist was smoking his last cigar, and the air grew thicker and thicker. Twice the Chief Inspector had gone out for a stroll through the building and had seen the two women in the waiting room. The second time, he saw that they'd drawn their chairs closer and were gossiping together as if they'd known each other for years.

"When did you clean your car?"

"It was last cleaned two weeks ago, in a garage in Neuilly, at the same time they changed the oil."

"It hasn't been cleaned again since Sunday?"

"No."

"You see, Monsieur Serre, we've just performed a decisive experiment. One of my men, who, like you, has rubber heels, drove out to the place you marked on the Fontaine-bleau road. As you stated that you did on Sunday with your mother, he got out of the car and went for a walk along the country lane, which wasn't paved. He got back in the car and returned here.

"The experts from our laboratory, who are supposed to know their job, then examined the mat in the car.

"Here is the dirt and gravel they found."

He pushed a small paper bag across the desk.

Serre made no move to take it.

"We would have found the same thing on the mat in your car."

"That proves I killed my wife?"

"It proves that your car has been cleaned since Sunday."

"Couldn't someone have got into my garage?"

"It's unlikely."

"Didn't your men get in?"

"What are you insinuating?"

"Nothing, Chief Inspector. I'm not accusing anyone. I'm merely pointing out to you that this operation was under-taken without witnesses, therefore without legal standing."

138

"Wouldn't you like to speak to your mother?"

"You'd love to know what I would have to say to her, wouldn't you? Nothing, Monsieur Maigret. I have nothing to say to her, and she has nothing to say to me."

A thought suddenly crossed his mind.

"Has she had anything to eat?"

"I can only repeat that she's a free agent."

"She won't leave as long as I'm here."

"She may be in for a long stay."

Serre lowered his eyes, and his manner seemed to change. After a long hesitation, he muttered, as if slightly ashamed: "I suppose it would be asking too much to have a sandwich sent in to her?"

"That was done a long time ago."

"Did she eat it?"

"Yes."

"How is she?"

"She's busy talking."

"To whom?"

"To a certain person who's also in the waiting room—a girl who used to be on the streets."

Again there was a gleam of hate in the dentist's eyes.

"You arranged that deliberately, didn't you?"

"No."

"My mother has nothing to tell."

"All the better for you."

They spent the next quarter of an hour in silence. Then Maigret plodded into the next room, glummer than ever, and motioned to Janvier, who was dozing in a corner.

"Same routine, Chief?"

"Anything you like."

139

The stenographer was worn out. The translator was still typing.

"Go get Ernestine, the one with the green hat, and take her to Lucas's office."

When Lofty came in, she didn't look pleased.

"You shouldn't have interrupted us. She'll start suspecting something."

Perhaps because it was late at night, Maigret spoke to her more familiarly than usual, without noticing it.

"What've you been telling her?"

"How I didn't know why I'd been made to come here, how my husband's been missing two days and I'd had no news, how much I hate the police and the tricks they're always playing.

" 'They're just keeping me waiting here to try to shake me!' I told her. 'They think they can get away with anything.' "

"What did she say?"

"She asked me if I'd been here before. I said yes, I'd been put through it for a whole night, a year ago, because my husband had had a fight in a café and they wanted to make out he'd knifed somebody. . . . At first, she looked at me like she was disgusted. Then little by little she began to ask me questions."

"What?"

"Mostly about you. I told her everything bad I could think up. I made sure to add that you always managed to make people talk, however tough you had to get with them."

"What!"

"I know what I'm doing. . . . I told her about the time

140

you kept somebody stark naked in your office for twenty-four hours, in midwinter, and made sure the window was wide open."

"That never happened!"

"Well, it shook her. She's less sure of herself than she was when I got here. She spends all her time listening."

" 'Does he beat people?' she asked me.

" 'It's been known.'

"Would you like me to go back to her?" Ernestine finally asked the Chief Inspector.

"If you want to."

"Only, I'd like to be taken back to the waiting room by one of your men, and have him be rough with me."

"Still no news of Alfred?"

"You haven't had any either?"

Maigret had her taken back in the way she'd asked for, and the Inspector returned grinning wryly.

"What happened?"

"Nothing much. When I went past the old girl, she put up her arm as if she thought I was going to hit her. And just as I was leaving the room, Lofty burst out crying."

Madame Maigret called to find out if her husband had eaten anything.

"Shall I wait for you?"

"Certainly not."

He had a headache. He was disgruntled, with himself, with everybody. He was a little uneasy, as well. He wondered what would happen if they suddenly received a telephone call from Maria Van Aerts, announcing that she'd changed her plans and had quietly settled down in some town or other.

141

He drank a glass of beer, now tepid, and asked somebody to get more sent up before the brasserie closed. Back in his office, he saw that Janvier had opened the window. The clamor of the city had subsided, and only now and then did a taxi cross Pont St.-Michel.

He sat down, his shoulders drooping. Janvier went out.

After a long pause, he said, musingly: "Your mother's got it into her head that I'm torturing you."

He was surprised to see the other raise his head sharply; for the first time, he saw the face look anxious.

"What have they been telling her?"

"I don't know. It's probably the girl in there with her. Some people like to make up stories, to seem more interesting."

"May I see her?"

"Who?"

"My mother."

Maigret pretended to hesitate, to weigh the pros and cons. Finally he shook his head.

"No," he said decisively. "I think I'll question her myself. And I'm wondering if I shouldn't bring Eugénie here, too."

"My mother doesn't know anything."

"Do you?"

"I don't either."

"Then there's no reason why I shouldn't question her as I've questioned you."

"Haven't you any pity, Chief Inspector?"

"For whom?"

"An old woman."

"Maria would have liked to become an old woman, too."

142

He walked up and down, his hands behind his back, but what he was waiting for didn't come.

"Your turn, Janvier! I'm going to have a crack at the mother."

Actually, he didn't know yet whether he would do that or not. Janvier said later that he'd never known the Chief to be so tired and so surly as he was that night.

It was one in the morning. Everybody in the PJ had lost confidence; chagrined glances were exchanged behind the Chief Inspector's back.

8

Maigret was leaving the duty room, on his way to look in on the translator, when one of the cleaners, who had invaded the building half an hour before, came up to tell him: "There's someone asking to speak to you."

"Where?"

"It's one of the two in the waiting room. Seems she's not feeling well. She came into the office I was sweeping out, white in the face, like she was sick, and asked me to get you."

"The old lady?" Maigret asked, frowning.

"No, the younger one."

Most of the doors along the corridor were open. In an office two doors down, the Chief Inspector saw Ernestine, holding one hand to her breast. He moved quickly forward, scowling, his lips framing a question.

"Shut the door," she whispered when he was within earshot.

And, as soon as he'd done so, she explained.

"Phew! I couldn't stick it any longer. That's the truth. But I'm not sick. I put on an act, so's I could get away from her for a while. . . . Not that I'm feeling any too bright, though. You wouldn't have a drink around the place, would you?"

He had to go back to his office to get the bottle of brandy he always kept in the closet. Not having anything smaller, he poured some into a tumbler. She swallowed it at a gulp, with a shudder.

"I don't know how you're managing with the son, but the mother's got me down. I thought I'd go nuts."

"Did she talk?"

"She's smarter than me. That's what I wanted to tell you. . . . To start off, I made sure she'd swallowed all the stories I was stuffing her with.

"Then—I don't know how it happened—she started to pop in a question here and there, all innocence. I've been third-degreed before now, and I figured I could hold my own.

"With her, I didn't have a chance."

"Did you tell her what you were?"

"Not right away. That woman's very very clever, Monsieur Maigret. How could she have guessed I'd been on the street? Tell me, does it still show? . . .

"She says: 'You're no stranger to this kind of people, are you?'

145

"It was your fellows she was referring to.

"Finally, she's asking me what it's like in jail, and I'm telling her.

"If you'd said, when I sat down there in front of her, that I'd spill anything, I'd have refused to believe it."

"Did you tell her about Alfred?"

"In a way—without saying exactly what his game is. She's not that interested. . . . For three quarters of an hour now, at least, she's been asking me about life in jail: what time you get up, what you have to eat, what the guards are like. . . . I thought you'd be interested to know, so I made out I felt sick. I said I was going to ask for a drink, that it wasn't human to make women hang around all night. . . .

"Mind if I have another drop?"

She really was worn out. The brandy brought color back into her cheeks.

"Her son won't talk?"

"Not yet. Has she said anything about him?"

"She listens to every sound, jumps every time a door opens. . . . Something else she asked me: she wanted to know if I'd met anybody who'd got the guillotine. . . . Well, I feel better now. I'll go back to her. But I'll be on my guard this time, don't worry."

She took the opportunity to put on some powder, and looked at the bottle, but didn't venture to ask for a third drink.

"What's the time?"

"Three o'clock."

"I don't know how she sticks it. She doesn't look tired, and she's sitting up as straight as ever."

Maigret let her out, took a breath of air at a window opening onto the courtyard, and swallowed a mouthful of brandy out of the bottle. As he went by the office where the translator was working, the man called to him to show him a passage he'd underlined in one of the letters.

"This dates back a year and a half," he said.

Maria had written to her friend:

Yesterday I had a good laugh. G. came to my room, not for what you might think, but to talk to me about an idea I'd proposed the day before: to spend a couple of days in Nice.

They're terrified of traveling, these people. Only once in their lives have they ever been out of France. That one trip abroad goes back to the time when the father was still alive and they all went over to London together. Incidentally, it appears that they were all seasick and had to call in the ship's doctor.

But that's neither here nor there.

Whenever I say something that doesn't suit them, they don't answer right away. They just stop talking, and, as the saying goes, you can hear a pin drop.

Well, the next day, G. comes to my room, looking distressed, beats around the bush, finally confesses what's worrying him. Briefly, it seems that my idea of going to Nice for the Carnival was ludicrous, almost indecent. He made no bones about telling me that his mother had been shocked by it and pleaded with me to give up the idea.

It so happened that the drawer of my bedside table was open. He glanced into it, and I saw him turn pale.

"What's that?" he stammered, pointing at the little automatic with mother-of-pearl that I bought during my trip to Egypt.

147

Do you remember? I wrote to you about it at the time. People had told me that a woman on her own was never safe in places like that.

I don't know why I'd put it in that drawer. I said, coolly: "It's a pistol."

"Is it loaded?"

"I don't remember."

I picked it up, looked in the magazine. There were no bullets in it.

"Have you any ammunition?" he asked.

"There must be some somewhere."

Half an hour later, my mother-in-law came in on some excuse; she never enters my room without giving a reason. She also beat around the bush for a while, then explained to me that it was most unseemly for a woman to carry firearms.

"But it's more like a toy," I said. "I keep it as a souvenir, because the handle's pretty and my initials are on it. I don't think it could harm anybody."

She stopped fussing finally. But not before I'd given her the box of ammunition, which was in the bottom of a drawer.

The funny part is that no sooner had she gone than I found in one of my handbags another box of ammunition, which I'd forgotten about. I didn't tell her. . . .

Maigret, who was holding the brandy bottle in his hand, poured some for the translator, then went to give some to the stenographer and an inspector who, to try to keep awake, was doodling on his blotter.

When he went back into his office, which Janvier vacated automatically, the bell sounded for another round.

———

"I've been thinking, Serre. . . . I'm beginning to believe that you haven't been lying as much as I supposed."

He'd dropped the "Monsieur," as if so many hours alone together had brought a sort of familiarity. The dentist merely regarded him mistrustfully.

"Maria wasn't meant to disappear, any more than your first wife. Her disappearance wasn't to your advantage. She'd packed her bags, announced her departure for Holland. She really intended to take the night train.

"I don't know if she was supposed to die in the house or not until she got outside. What do you say to that?"

Guillaume Serre made no reply, but his expression betrayed much more concern.

"If you like it better, let's say she was meant to die a natural death, by which I mean a death that would *pass as natural.*

"This didn't happen. If it had, you'd have had no reason to dispose of her body or her luggage.

"There's another thing that doesn't add up. You'd said good-bye to each other, so she had no reason to go into your study. Yet her dead body was there at a certain time that night. . . .

"I'm not asking you to answer me, but to follow my reasoning. . . . I've just found out that your wife owned a pistol.

"I'm ready to believe that you shot her in self-defense. After that, you panicked. You left the body where it had fallen while you went to get your car out of the garage. It was then, around midnight, that the concierge saw you.

"What I'm trying to figure out is what changed both your plans and hers. You were in your study, weren't you?"

"I don't remember."

"That's what you stated."

"Possibly."

"I'm convinced that your mother was not in her room, but with you."

"She was in her room."

"So you remember that?"

"Yes."

"Then you remember, also, that you were in your study? Your wife hadn't gone out to get a taxi yet. If she'd brought one back that night, we'd have found the driver. In other words, it was before leaving the house that she changed her mind and went to your study. Why?"

"I have no idea."

"You admit that she went there to see you?"

"No."

"You're being unwise, Serre. There are very few instances, in criminal records, when a dead body hasn't been found sooner or later. We'll find hers. And I'm certain, now, that a postmortem will reveal that she was killed by one or several bullet wounds. What I'm wondering is whether it was a shot fired by your gun or a shot fired by hers.

"The seriousness of your case will depend on that. If the bullet came from her pistol, the conclusion will be drawn that, for one reason or another, she took it into her head to go and settle some score with you, to threaten you.

"Money perhaps, Serre?"

He shrugged.

"You leaped at her, disarmed her, and squeezed the trigger without meaning to.

"Another theory could be that she threatened your mother, not you. A woman's more likely to feel hatred for another woman than for a man.

"A final possibility is that your revolver was not in your room, where you put it soon after, but in the drawer of your desk.

"Maria comes in. She's armed. She threatens you. You pull the drawer open and shoot first.

"In any case, you're in no danger of execution. There can be no question of premeditation, since it's quite normal to keep a pistol in the desk of one's study.

"You can even plead self-defense.

"What remains to be explained is why your wife, on the point of leaving, should suddenly have rushed in to see you with a gun in her hand."

Maigret leaned back and slowly filled a pipe, without taking his eyes off Serre.

"What do you say to that?"

"This can go on forever," Serre said, in a tone of disgust.

"You still refuse to talk?"

"I'm answering your questions obediently."

"You haven't told me why you shot her."

"I didn't shoot her."

"Then your mother did?"

"My mother didn't shoot her either. She was up in her room."

"While you were quarreling with your wife?"

"There was no quarrel."

"Pity."

"I'm so sorry."

"You see, Serre, I've done my best to discover any reason

151

your wife may have had for settling accounts with you and threatening you."

"She didn't threaten me."

"Don't be too positive about it, because you may regret it later on. It's you who will plead with me or with the jury to believe that your life or your mother's was in danger."

Serre smiled sardonically. He was tired, slumped down, his shoulders slightly hunched around his neck, but he hadn't lost any of his self-possession. His beard showed blue through the skin on his cheeks. The sky, beyond the windowpanes, was by now not quite so dark, and the air in the room was becoming cooler.

It was Maigret who felt the cold first. He went over to close the window.

"It wasn't to your advantage to have a corpse on your hands. I mean *a corpse that nobody could be allowed to see.* Do you follow me?"

"No."

"When your first wife died, it was in such a manner that you were able to call in Dr. Dutilleux to make out the death certificate.

"That's how Maria was supposed to die, from apparently natural causes. She had a weak heart, too. What had worked once could work again.

"But something went wrong.

"Do you see, now, what I'm getting at?"

"I didn't kill her."

"And you didn't dispose of her body, and her luggage and the burglar's tools?"

"There wasn't any burglar."

"I'll probably confront you with him in a few hours."

"You've found him?"

His tone was slightly uneasy.

"We were able to find his fingerprints in your study. You were careful to wipe the furniture, but there's always some piece that gets forgotten. . . . He happens to be an old offender, an expert, in his way, well known here: Alfred Jussiaume—'Sad Freddie,' they call him. He told his wife what he'd seen. She is now out there in the waiting room with your mother. As for Jussiaume, he's in Rouen and has no further reason to remain in hiding.

"We already have the concierge who saw you take your car out of the garage. We've also got the hardware-shop clerk who sold you a second pane of glass at eight o'clock on Wednesday morning.

"The laboratory can prove that your car has been cleaned since then.

"That makes quite a lot of evidence, doesn't it?

"When we've found the body and the luggage, my job will be over.

"Then, perhaps, you'll decide to explain why, instead of a, shall we say, lawful corpse, you found yourself saddled with a body that you had to dispose of at once.

"There was some hitch.

"What was it, Serre?"

The man pulled a handkerchief out of his pocket, wiped his lips and forehead, but didn't open his mouth to reply.

"It's half past three. I'm beginning to get fed up. Are you still determined not to talk?"

"I have nothing to say."

153

"Very well," said Maigret, getting up. "I don't like having to bully an old woman, but I see I'm forced to question your mother."

He expected a protest, or at least some display of feeling. The dentist didn't move, however, and it seemed to Maigret that he even showed a kind of relief, that his nerves relaxed.

"You take over, Janvier. I'll get busy on the mother."

That really was his intention, but he was unable to carry it out immediately. Vacher had just appeared, in great excitement, a package in his hand.

"I've got it, Chief! Took me some time, but I think this is it."

He unwrapped an old newspaper to reveal broken bits of brick and some reddish dust.

"Where?"

"On Quai de Billancourt, opposite the Ile Séguin. If I'd started downstream, instead of upstream, I'd have been here hours ago. I've been over all the docks where they unload. Billancourt was the only place where a barge had unloaded bricks lately."

"When?"

"Last Monday. It left about noon on Tuesday. The bricks are still there, and boys must have been playing there, because quite a lot of them have been broken. There's a red dust covering a good bit of the quay. . . . Shall I take it up to Moers?"

"I'll go myself."

As he went by the waiting room, he looked at the two women sitting there. It seemed, from their attitudes, as if there was now a chill between them.

154

Maigret entered the laboratory, where he felt he'd earned a cup of the coffee Moers had just made.

"Have you got that sample of brick dust? Like to compare it with this?"

Moers used magnifiers, slides, and a projector. The color was the same; the structure seemed identical.

"Does it add up?"

"Very likely. Comes from the same district, anyhow. It'll take me about thirty minutes to an hour to do the analysis."

It was too early to have the Seine dragged. The River Police wouldn't be able to send a diver down until after sunrise. Then, if they found Maria's body, or only the luggage and the tools, the circle would be closed.

"Hello! River Police? This is Maigret."

He still seemed to be in a bad temper.

"I'd like you to drag the Seine as soon as possible, Quai de Billancourt, the place where a load of bricks was delivered recently."

"In an hour from now, with daylight."

Why should he continue to wait? No jury would ask for further proof to find Guillaume Serre guilty, even if he persisted in his denials. Without paying any attention to the stenographer, who was staring at him, Maigret took a long pull at his bottle, wiped his mouth, went out into the corridor, and threw open the door of the waiting room.

Ernestine thought he'd come for her and sprang quickly to her feet. Madame Serre did not move.

It was the latter to whom Maigret spoke.

"Would you mind coming with me for a moment?"

There was a large choice of empty offices. He pushed open a door at random and closed the window.

"Please sit down."

He began to circle the room, glancing at the old lady sourly from time to time.

"I don't much like to break bad news," he growled at last. "Especially to someone your age. Have you ever been ill, Madame Serre?"

"Except when we were seasick, crossing the Channel, I've never had to call in the doctor."

"So, naturally, you don't suffer from heart trouble?"

"No."

"Your son does, however?"

"He's always had an enlarged heart."

"He killed his wife!" he shot out suddenly, raising his head and staring her in the face.

"Did he tell you so himself?"

He hated to use the old trick of a false confession.

"He still denies it, but that won't help. We've got proof."

"That he's a murderer?"

"That he shot Maria, in his study."

She had not moved, but her features had stiffened slightly. It was as though she had stopped breathing, but she showed no other sign of emotion.

"What proof have you?"

"We've found the spot where his wife's body was thrown into the river, with her luggage and the burglar's tools."

"Ah!"

That was all she said. She was waiting, her hands folded stiffly on her dark dress.

"Your son refuses to plead self-defense. That's a mistake; because I'm convinced that, when his wife entered the study, she was armed and meant to do him harm."

156

"Why?"

"That's what I'm asking you."

"I have no idea."

"Where were you?"

"In my room, as I told you."

"You didn't hear anything?"

"Nothing. Only the door closing. Then the sound of a car's engine, in the street."

"The taxi?"

"I thought it must be a taxi, since my daughter-in-law had said she was going to get one."

"You're sure? Might it not have been a private car?"

"I didn't see it."

"Then it might easily have been your son's car?"

"He swore to me that he didn't go out."

"You realize the discrepancy between what you're saying now and the statements you made to me when you came here of your own accord?"

"No."

"You stated positively that your daughter-in-law went away in a taxi."

"I still think she did."

"But you're no longer certain about it. Are you so certain now that there was no attempted burglary?"

"I saw no sign of any."

"What time did you go downstairs on Wednesday morning?"

"About half past six."

"Did you go into the study?"

"Not immediately. I got the coffee ready."

"You didn't go and open the shutters?"

"Yes, I believe so."

"Before your son came down?"

"Probably."

"You wouldn't swear to it?"

"Put yourself in my place, Monsieur Maigret. For two days I've hardly known where I am. I've been asked all sorts of questions. I've been sitting in your waiting room for I don't know how many hours. I'm tired. I'm doing my best to hold together."

"Why did you come here tonight?"

"Isn't it natural for a mother to follow her son in such circumstances? I've always lived with him. He might be in need of me."

"Would you follow him to prison?"

"I don't understand. I can't believe that—"

"Let me put it another way. If I charged your son, would you be willing to share the responsibility for what he did?"

"But he hasn't done anything!"

"Are you sure of that?"

"Why should he kill his wife?"

"You avoid giving me a straight answer. Are you convinced that he didn't kill her?"

"So far as I can tell."

"Is there any chance that he did so?"

"He had no reason to."

"But he did!" Maigret said harshly, staring her in the face again.

She sat as if in suspended animation.

"Ah!" she breathed, then opened her bag to take out her handkerchief. Her eyes were dry; she wasn't crying. She merely dabbed at her lips with the handkerchief.

158

"May I have a glass of water?"

He had to hunt around, since he didn't know the office as well as his own, before finding it for her.

"As soon as the Public Prosecutor arrives at the Palais de Justice, your son will be charged. I can tell you now that he hasn't the slightest chance of getting away with it."

"You mean that—"

"He'll go to the guillotine."

She didn't faint, but sat rigid on her chair, staring blankly.

"His first wife's body will be exhumed. I daresay you know that traces of certain poisons can be found in a skeleton."

"Why should he have killed them both? It isn't possible. It isn't true, Chief Inspector. I don't know why you're telling me this, but I refuse to believe you. Let me speak to him. Let me to talk to him in private, and I'll find out the truth."

"Were you in your room the whole of Tuesday evening?"

"Yes."

"You didn't go downstairs at all?"

"No. Why should I, when that woman was leaving us at last?"

Maigret went over to cool his forehead against the windowpane, then walked into the office next door, grabbed the bottle, and drank from it the equivalent of three or four singles.

When he came back, he had assumed the heavy gait of Guillaume Serre and his obstinate glare.

9

He was sitting in a chair that wasn't his, both elbows on the desk, his biggest pipe in his mouth, his eyes fixed upon the old lady he had thought looked like a mother superior.

"Your son, Madame Serre, didn't kill either his first or his second wife," he said, spacing out the words.

She frowned in surprise, but didn't look any happier.

"Nor did he kill his father," he added.

"What do you—"

"Quiet! . . . If you don't mind, we'll settle this as quickly as possible. We'll not bother about proof for the time being. That will come in due course.

"We won't argue about your husband's case, either. What

160

I'm almost certain of is that your first daughter-in-law was poisoned. I'll go further. I'm convinced that it wasn't done by arsenic or any of the strong poisons that are usually used.

"By the way, Madame Serre, I might tell you that, in nine cases out of ten, poison is a woman's weapon.

"Your first daughter-in-law, like the second, suffered from heart trouble. So did your husband.

"Certain drugs, which wouldn't seriously affect people in good health, can be fatal to cardiac cases. I wonder if Maria didn't provide us with the key to the problem in one of her letters to her friend. She speaks of a trip to England, which you once took with your husband, and emphasizes that you were all so badly seasick that you had to see the ship's doctor.

"What would be prescribed in such a case?"

"I have no idea."

"That's very unlikely. They usually give you atropine in some form or other. Now, a fairly strong dose of atropine can be fatal to a person with a weak heart."

"You mean that my husband—"

"We'll go into that another time, even if it's impossible to prove anything. Your husband, during his later days, was leading a disorderly life and throwing his money away. . . . You've always been afraid of poverty, Madame Serre."

"Not for myself. For my son. Which doesn't mean that I would have—"

"Later on, your son got married. Another woman came to live in your house, a woman who, overnight, bore your name and had as much right there as you did."

She compressed her lips.

"This woman, who also had a weak heart, was rich, richer than your son, richer than all the Serres put together."

"You believe that I poisoned her, having first poisoned my husband?"

"Yes."

She gave a little strained laugh.

"Doubtless I also poisoned my second daughter-in-law?"

"She was going away, discouraged, after having tried in vain to live in a house where she was treated like a stranger. Very likely she was taking her money with her. By a coincidence, she had heart trouble too.

"You see, I wondered from the beginning why her body disappeared. If she'd simply been poisoned, you had only to call in a doctor, who, given Maria's state of health, would have diagnosed a heart attack. Perhaps the attack itself was intended to come on later, in the taxi, at the station, or on the train."

"You seem very sure of yourself, Monsieur Maigret."

"I know that something happened that obliged your son to shoot his wife. Let's suppose that Maria, just as she was going to get a taxi, or, more likely, as she was on the point of telephoning for one, felt certain symptoms.

"She knew you both, having lived with you for two and a half years. She was a widely read woman, in all sorts of subjects, and it wouldn't surprise me to know that she had acquired some medical knowledge.

"Realizing that she'd been poisoned, she went into her husband's study, where you were with him."

"Why do you say I was there?"

"Because, unfortunately for her, she laid the blame on

162

you. If you'd been in your room, she'd have gone upstairs.

"I don't know if she threatened you with her pistol or if she merely reached for the telephone to call the police. . . .

"There was only one way out for you: to shoot her."

"And, according to you, it was I who—"

"No. I've already told you that it's more likely to have been your son who fired, or, if you'd rather, finished your work for you."

The drab light of dawn blended with the electric light, showing that the lines in their faces were etched more deeply. The telephone rang.

"That you, Chief? I've done the test. It's ten to one that the brick dust we found in the car came from Billancourt."

"You can go home to bed, my friend. Your job's finished."

He got up once again and circled the room.

"Your son, Madame Serre, is determined to shoulder all the blame. I don't see any way of keeping him from this. If he's been able to keep his mouth shut all this time, he's capable of keeping it shut for good. Unless—"

"Unless . . . ?"

"I don't know. I'm thinking aloud. Two years ago, I had a man as tough as he is in my office and, after fifteen hours, we still hadn't got a word out of him."

He threw open the window abruptly, in a kind of rage.

"It took twenty-seven and a half hours to break his nerve."

"Did he confess?"

"He spilled everything in one long stream, as if it were a relief to get rid of it."

"I didn't poison anybody."

163

"The answer doesn't lie with you."

"With my son?"

"Yes. He's convinced that you did it only for his sake, partly out of fear that he'd be left penniless, partly out of jealousy."

He had to restrain himself from raising his hand to her, despite her age, for the old woman's thin lips had just twitched in an involuntary smile.

"Which is a lie!" he said flatly.

Then, coming closer to her, his eyes on hers, his breath on her face, he rapped out:

"It's not for his sake that you're afraid of poverty; it's for your own! It's not for his sake that you murdered; you came here tonight because you were afraid he might talk."

She tried to shrink away from Maigret's face, thrust into hers, hard, menacing.

"Never mind if he does go to prison, or even if he's executed, so long as you can be sure of staying in the clear. You believe you still have many years to live, in your house, counting your money. . . ."

She was frightened. Her mouth opened as if to call for help. Suddenly, with a violent unexpected jerk, Maigret wrenched from her withered hands the bag she was clinging to.

She gave a cry and shot forward to retrieve it.

"Sit down."

He undid the silver clasp. Right at the bottom, beneath the gloves, the wallet, the handkerchief, and the powder compact, he found a folded paper that contained two white pills.

A hush like that in a church or a cavern enclosed them. Maigret let his body relax, then pressed the bell.

When the door opened, he said slowly, without a glance at the Inspector who'd appeared: "Tell Janvier to stop his questioning."

And, as the Inspector still stood there looking amazed: "It's all over. She's confessed."

"I haven't confessed to anything."

He waited until the door closed.

"It comes to the same thing. I could have carried the experiment to its end—let you have the private talk with your son that you wanted. . . . Don't you think you've caused enough deaths already for one old woman?"

"You mean that I would have—"

He was toying with the pills.

"You'd have given him his medicine—or what he would have thought was his medicine—and there would have been no danger of his ever talking again."

The roofs had begun to be crested with sunlight. The telephone rang again.

"Chief Inspector Maigret? This is the River Police. We're at Billancourt. The diver's just gone down for the first time, and he's found a pretty heavy trunk."

"The rest'll turn up too!" he said indifferently.

An exhausted and astonished Janvier was standing in the doorway.

"They told me—"

"Take her down to the cells. The man, too, as an accessory. I'll see the Public Prosecutor as soon as he comes in."

165

He no longer had any business with either the mother or the son.

"You can go to bed," he told the translator.

"It's over?"

"For today."

The dentist was no longer there when he entered his office, but the ashtray was full of very black cigar butts. He sat down in his chair, and was about to doze off, when he remembered Lofty.

He found her asleep in the waiting room and shook her by the shoulder. Instinctively, she straightened her green hat.

"That's it. Off you go now."

"Has he confessed?"

"It was her."

"What! It was the old girl who—"

"Later!" he murmured.

Then, assailed by a twinge of remorse, he turned around and said: "Thanks! When Alfred comes back, advise him to—"

But what good would that do? Nothing would cure Sad Freddie of his mania for burgling the safes he had once installed, or wean him from his belief that each would be the last, that this time he was really going to live in the country.

Because of her age, old Madame Serre was not executed. She left the court with the complacent air of one who is at last going to set the women's prison in order.

When her son came out of Fresnes, after two years, he

166

went right to the house on rue de la Ferme. That very evening, he took his usual stroll around the neighborhood, the one he took in the days when he had a dog to exercise.

He continued to go and drink red wine in the little bistro, and, before entering, to look uneasily up and down the street.

Shadow Rock Farm
Lakeville, Connecticut